AMBUSH CANYON

AMBUSH CANYON

Lauran Paine

Chivers Press • G.K. Hall & Co.
Bath, England Waterville, Maine USA

This Large Print edition is published by Chivers Press, England, and by G.K. Hall & Co., USA.

Published in 2001 in the U.K. by arrangement with Robert Hale Limited.

Published in 2001 in the U.S. by arrangement with Golden West Literary Agency.

U.K. Hardcover   ISBN 0-7540-4667-2   (Chivers Large Print)
U.K. Softcover   ISBN 0-7540-4668-0   (Camden Large Print)
U.S. Softcover   ISBN 0-7838-9478-3   (Nightingale Series Edition)

The text of this Large Print edition is unabridged.
Other aspects of the book may vary from the original edition.

Set in 16 pt. New Times Roman.

Printed in Great Britain on acid-free paper.

British Library Cataloguing in Publication Data available

Library of Congress Cataloging-in-Publication Data

Paine, Lauran.
    Ambush Canyon / by Lauran Paine.
      p.   cm.
    ISBN 0-7838-9478-3 (lg. print : sc : alk. paper)
    1. Large type books.
    PS3566.A34 A8 2001
    813'.54—dc21   2001039238

CHAPTER ONE

Old Jim Morton surveyed the others standing in his ranch yard, the five of them looking uncomfortable, and said with booming contempt, 'The law! The hell with the law, I got something better, I got power!'

And Jim's pardner, thin Buckley Fisk with his deaths-head face and perpetual look of saturnine scorn, said in a quieter voice but with its own variety of deadliness to it, 'We've gone along; all of us have gone along. But there's got to be an end and this is it. The next herd that comes through the canyon gets a full dose, and either you're with us or you're not. But if you're not, men, then I promise you one thing. When we turn 'em off at the pass they'll spread out over *your* land, not ours.'

The other five looked back and forth and stood awkwardly uncertain, stood restless, made that way by indecision. One of them eventually said to Morton in a roughened voice, 'We can't go against the law, Jim.'

'Why not?' demanded big old Jim Morton. 'I'd like you to tell me why not. Who made this damned country—us or the law? Who wiped out the redskins and chased off the thieves and killers? Who made this a cowmans' land? *We* did! Buck and me and the rest of you, an' now you stand there shrinkin' from a hangin' or

1

two, a little shootin' of a bunch of scum drivin' cattle up out of the Panhandle over our range like they had the right, and eatin' our grass down into dust.'

Big Jim spat through his teeth and glared. He was on the sundown side of fifty years and for half that time when Big Jim Morton had said jump, folks didn't ask where, they said how high? He was over six feet tall with a florid face, a high paunch, two massive fists, and two little greeny eyes that looked straight to the core of any situation. He was in most things the direct opposite of Buckley Fisk, who had been his pardner for twenty-two years.

Buckley was under fifty but as leathery and lined as a much older man might have been. And Buckley was as skinny as a rail to Big Jim's massive heaviness. But Buckley and Jim thought the same way and they were nearly the same height, except that Buckley Fisk always seemed much taller because of his emaciated thinness. Buckley had never been much with his fists like Jim had been, but he was deadly with guns, so they complemented one another. Years back someone had said that when an enemy of Fisk or Morton had a choice between riding over MF range or through Comanche country, if he had a particle of sense he took his chances with the Comanches.

But there was more.

In the days when Morton and Fisk were putting together their huge holdings land was cheap and worthless, so if Big Jim Morton slyly winked and bought the drinks, and afterwards worked fraud to gain title to the Indian lands, folks chuckled and wagged their heads and said Morton and Fisk were truly a pair, indeed they were, and no one cared because no one, in those early times, thought that land would ever be worth a plugged cent. But Jim and Buckley had possessed the vast shrewdness of all robber-barons; *they* had known, so now they were the biggest, richest, most powerful cattlemen in Oklahoma's southwestern territory.

But it took a crew of tough men to patrol all that land, work all those MF cattle, and that was what Jim had meant when he'd said he had the power. He hired them cheap, fed them well, lent them the prestige of working for Fisk and Morton's mighty MF outfit, and when there was trouble shrewd and calculating old Jim could raffishly smile, and his ten cowboys would have charged the gates of hell itself if he'd wanted them to. Big Jim was a user of men; if there'd been a town worthy of the name closer than seventeen miles, or if his desires had lain in that direction, Big Jim could have been a mayor or a governor, or the boss of a ring of unethical feeders at the public trough. He was that kind of a man: cold, inwardly dispassionate, inwardly as unemotional as a block of ice, but very clever, very wise in the ways of men;

3

always willing upon a moment's notice to show his blustery, forceful side to win friends and influence other men, but never, never, letting anyone know exactly what was in his mind.

So he stood there playing those five cowmen in his yard as a cat plays with baby mice, alternately shaming them, cajoling them, figuratively patting them upon the back, and putting rings in their noses to lead them by.

'I tell you for a fact,' he boomed at them. 'Let one drought hit us after them drovers have taken our grass, and we're through, finished, wiped out. And, boys, we get droughts out here in the short-grass country. Buckley an' I've seen many a bad year. But we pulled through because we rationed the grass. Now then, what do you say; do we let them lousy Texans ruin us, or do we teach 'em respect for our rights?'

Buckley Fisk jumped in ahead of any answers those men might have given. Buckley said in his reedy twang: 'You're worryin' about the law. Let me tell you, boys, we *are* the law. We been the law for a quarter century. Where was them federal marshals and sheriffs and soldiers when the Comanches was shootin' us down at night by the lamps of our own sittin' rooms? I'll tell you where—in some stinkin' town or fort drinkin' whiskey and playin' cards! The same place they are right now. What do they care whether or not we survive? They *don't* care! We're the only ones who care—and we're the law!'

Those five cattlemen stood there looking glum and undecided still; looking fretful about the half-truths. One of them was Carleton Whitney whose neighbours considered a solid man of sound judgement. Whitney was perhaps forty although, as with all men of his outdoor kind, he could have been ten years older or five years younger. He hitched at his shell-belt and said, 'You may be right,' to Jim Morton, 'but what I'm thinkin' is that if we shoot up one of those outfits it won't make 'em as careful as it'll make 'em vengeful. And Jim, you want to remember, they're mostly Texans.'

Buckley Fisk burned them with his scorn. 'Texans! Let 'em *be* Texans! Let 'em be anything they got to be, only teach 'em manners; teach 'em the only way men understand, that when they bring herds over our land, they're goin' to lose some men an' some cattle.'

Whitney sank into troubled silence. None of the others wished to be singed by deaths-head Buckley Fisk's contempt, so they too were silent.

Then Big Jim hooked thumbs in his vest at the armpits and turned beamingly benevolent. He broadly smiled down upon them, he showed his three front gold teeth and puckered up his greeny eyes until they were hidden in mounds of flesh. He turned smooth and placating and compassionate towards

5

them. 'Listen; I know how you feel. Who wants to ride out an' deliberately kill men we don't even know? Hell; there's probably a lot of them fellers that're the salt of the earth. Family men with kids down in Texas maybe. Nice fellers to have a drink with. All right, boys; let's do it this way then. Let's ride out to Ambush Canyon, halt the next herd where it comes down the pass, and turn it back, an' if they make trouble for us, why then we'll pass the word to our riders—when you shoot, if you got to, aim low; set 'em afoot or bust a leg here an' there—but no killing. How's that sound?'

The others looked sideways at Whitney, unwilling to speak themselves but willing Carleton to say what was in his mind, what was in all their minds. Whitney did, after an uncomfortable interval of silence had run out. He said, 'Well; that's better'n massacrin' 'em. But it still seems to me we're obliged to put the thing in Marshal Fulton's lap first. Then, if he don't do anything, why then I expect we'd be justified in protectin' ourselves.'

Buckley Fisk would have answered Whitney. His eyes were smoulderingly narrowed against the other man and his bloodless slash of a mouth was pulled downward. But Jim beat him to it.

'Fine,' boomed Big Jim. 'Fair enough. Carleton; you ride to town and explain the whole thing to Fulton. The rest of us'll hang an' rattle until you get back. Maybe we could

6

meet here again day after tomorrow. How's that?'

The others nodded and looked around and nodded some more. Whitney removed his hat, mopped sweat off his pale forehead, minutely examined the crown of that hat and stood a moment in long thought before he very carefully framed some words and very carefully spoke them. 'Jim; there's bound to be a question raised, if this thing ever amounts to anything, about land titles.'

Big Jim's greeny stare lingered upon Whitney. Big Jim as well as all the others knew what it was Whitney was having trouble putting into words. Morton and Fisk had Indian grants to much of their range, but the government didn't recognise such titles, and wisely too, because more often than not they had been procured while a cocked pistol had been held to some Indian's temple. Or at best, that land had been acquired for a wagon-load of flour, or perhaps ten or twelve rifles with mealy powder and unbalanced lead-slug bullets.

But Big Jim was equal to that too. He said blandly, 'All right; let someone raise that question, Carleton. MF's got its titles. But even if it didn't have, it'd still have squatters' rights. After all, Buckley an' me have been on our land longer'n anyone else in the country; we developed it, made it valuable. And we've held it too. So let someone bring up the matter of title. We'll see how far they get.'

There was solid warning in those words which did not escape a single man there in MF's yard. They'd all heard the old rumours of men drifting on to MF range with the means and the intention to settle there; men who were never afterwards heard of again as though the land had opened up and swallowed them.

'Well,' said Whitney lamely, replacing his hat. 'I just figured, since we're all in this together, wasn't any point in us not understandin' one another, Jim.'

Morton's expansive smile jumped up again. His three gold teeth wickedly reflected dazzling sunlight. 'Naturally,' he boomed at Whitney. 'An' that's the way things got to be, too. Everythin' out in the open.' He paused, then said, 'When you figure to ride into town and see Marshal Fulton?'

'Oh; I expect I'll head out from home before sunup in the morning.'

'Good,' beamed Big Jim. 'Fine. I like a man who makes up his mind, then does things. All right, boys; we'll meet here day after tomorrow to hear what Carleton's got to report.'

The five ranchers agreed to this and went after their horses leaving Morton and Fisk standing over there in barnshade silently watching them depart. They threw casual waves as was the custom, then turned and slowly paced towards their fort-like main

8

house, which stood perhaps twenty feet from the combination ranch dining-room and cookhouse. Because neither of them had ever married they ate with their hired hands, and because neither of them had ever ceased being working cattlemen, not even after affluence had come, they dressed and talked and acted like anyone else who lived in the raw, rough world of cattle and horses, flashfloods, gunfire, sere summers and bitter winters.

But they didn't *think* like that, which was what made them different and set them apart. 'Let 'em salve their consciences,' said Jim to Buckley as they stepped along towards the cookhouse. 'Let 'em go talk to that fool Bob Fulton. He won't do anything; he never does, so they'll come back in a week or two complainin' again about the trail-herds eating their grass. Then we'll lead 'em out. No more talkin' like we done today, Buck. Next time we lead 'em out.'

Fisk said serenely, 'I like what you said yesterday, Jim. I like the idea of usin' them fellers to make those drovers hunt a new northward trail, instead of us doin' all the fightin'.'

Big Jim chuckled. 'A few of them Texans'll get killed. You know the breed, Buck. No one tells 'em what to do. There'll be shooting, sure; but *we* won't do it. Whitney an' the others will. Why should we get involved if they'll clear the range for us?' Morton looked at the cookhouse dead ahead and said, 'Come on; let's get a cup of coffee.'

CHAPTER TWO

Bob Fulton at thirty-five was darkly handsome, quick as a cat, moody and at his best after he'd had two or three belts of Old Overholt. He wasn't really a drinker, but there seemed to be something inside Fulton which required appeasing from time to time. Still; he'd been stationed in Ione, Oklahoma Territory, four years, and so far no one had ever seen him drunk, which was perhaps just as well because towns as few and far between as Oklahoma possessed in Fulton's day, had plenty of fast guns not the least bit averse to chalking up a good clean kill of a U.S. Marshal. Nothing quite exalted a gunfighter's prestige as having a U.S. Marshal chalked up as a clean kill, and all that meant was that he couldn't be shot in the back, it had to be face-on, but if the marshal was drunk, that wasn't too derogatory because a lot of drunk men were more dangerous in that condition than when they were sober.

Fulton detested southern Oklahoma. He was a native of Arizona from up around Flagstaff, and he didn't like the rolling south plains country. He didn't like the people either, who were either transplanted Texans, a breed of men he viewed as congenital rebels, or else they were grave, quiet men with wary eyes who might have come from anywhere in a hurry.

He rarely mixed into the local feuds, spent most of his time at Ione, and prayerfully awaited the time when there would be a departmental shake-up and he would be transferred back to Arizona.

When Carleton Whitney met him on the sidewalk in front of Ab Slaughter's *Pecos Saloon* and offered to buy the drinks, Fulton knew something was in the wind. He accepted Whitney's offer, trooped on in behind Whitney and bellied up to Ab's bar. He didn't say anything even after their drinks came, and for a while he thought Whitney wasn't going to say anything either. It took a second straight shot to loosen the cowman's tongue, then it was about what Marshal Fulton had expected because he'd heard rumours of resentment among the westerly cowmen over trail-herds using their ranges.

But Bob Fulton hardened himself against intervention as long as he thought all Whitney wanted was for him to ride out the next time a herd came through, and detour it. His premature resolve altered when Whitney said MF was involved; said Morton and Fisk were for turning back the Texans with arms and mounted men. He knew those two; knew they

11

would do exactly as they said, so it now occurred to him that if there was riding to be done, he wouldn't have to go hunt some will-o-the-wisp Texas drovers, he'd have to go to MF and explain a few elemental facts of cow-country life, one of which was that no one took the law into their own hands. No one; and that also meant Morton and Fisk, the largest, richest, and most powerful cattlemen in southwestern Oklahoma Territory.

Then Whitney said something that made Fulton think. He said, 'Big Jim said if there was trouble when we rode out to turn the next herd back, all we'd have to do is shoot a few horses and bust a leg or two, for them drovers to get the idea.'

That, Fulton told himself as he leaned there at Ab's bar turning his little sticky shot-glass, had all the earmarks of a damned devious remark. Old Jim Morton knew a lot better than that and Whitney should also have known better; you didn't shoot up a drover-camp and just turn around and ride away.

'Give me a refill,' called Marshal Fulton down the bar, shoving his glass forward. 'How about you, Whitney?'

'No thanks.' Whitney stood there looking glum. He watched Fulton toss off his third straight shot with hopeless eyes. He was gazing at the marshal as though he expected this little talk to end in nothing, and he'd ridden seventeen miles, had another seventeen miles

12

to ride back, then eight more miles to ride in the morning to meet the others at MF—where he would have to report failure.

'Let me tell you something,' said Marshal Fulton, finally, turning that little glass again without looking around. 'Wars are fought by men who are told by other men what they got to do. These other men, they sort of lead the soldiers along to where their opposites on the other side have also arranged to have their soldiers. Then there's a big fight, Whitney; a lot of men die, but never the ones who sit up there on a hill watchin' and givin' the orders.'

Whitney was a forthright, honest man. He was not a clever nor a discerning man, so all this kind of talk went over his head, and what little impression it made at all was to confirm his earlier suspicion that he'd made that damned long ride for nothing. Still, he stood on, watching Fulton and listening to him. His horse was being grained over at the liverybarn, wouldn't be finished for another half hour and Whitney had nothing else to do in town, so he stood there.

'That's what's called using men, Whitney,' said Marshal Fulton, standing there all loose and relaxed playing with his empty glass. 'The big men of this world got that knack. The little men don't have it—so they're always the soldiers.' Fulton pushed the glass aside, straightened up and swung around. 'You understand what I'm drivin' at?'

13

Whitney said candidly, 'No. Unless you mean them Texans are using us by grazing over our grasslands.'

Marshal Fulton sighed. He wore a Prince Albert coat that was always tucked under his hip-holster on the right side where his ivory-butted .45 sagged outwards from his body making a convenient hand rest. He rested his hand upon that ivory stock now while he steadily gazed from dark, grave eyes at the cattleman.

He could have spelt it out for Whitney, but he didn't. He instead resigned himself to the long ride out to MF and the unpleasantness which was sure to ensue out there when he laid down the law to that old deaths-head and his beefy old pardner. You didn't attack a rattlesnake by cutting off his tail; you went for his head, which was how this thing had to be handled. You didn't bother with the Whitneys or even the Texas drovers. You went instead right to the heart of the trouble—which was MF.

'Care for another drink?' Fulton quietly asked.

Whitney shook his head, his face getting long. 'I'd like to fetch back word to the others what you figure to do,' he said.

Fulton nodded. 'All right. You tell your friends until I'm satisfied they got range-rights, I figure to do nothing. An' you also tell them that if they got a lick of sense, they'll do nothing too, because as near as I can figure out there's no law being broken, but if they do anything as foolish as buckin' a band of Texas drovers, there'll not only be laws broken, there'll also be some funerals.' Fulton drew up off the bar. 'And Whitney, one more thing; don't let Fisk or Morton push you into something you'll regret.'

'Marshal; we got range-rights. All my neighbours got government patents on their land.'

'Fisk and Morton too?'

Whitney's face clouded. 'I can't answer for them, Marshal, but you can look it up in the records.'

'I already have, Whitney. That was one of the first things I did when I came here—look up the land titles, because you see, until the government decides who's got legal right to Indian land in Oklahoma Territory, everyone is just squatting.'

Whitney glanced at the floor, his face troubled. For a moment Fulton looked at him thinking that this man and the hundreds like him were the backbone of Oklahoma; they were the unimaginative, forthright, honest, plodding men who worked from the dawn of their lives to its sundown time never achieving any greatness but always contributing to the solid base of a sovereignty. They were easily influenced and easily led, yet Fulton couldn't find it in his heart to condemn them because

15

whatever they did or tried to do, was in the sincere belief that they were doing right.

Still though, Fulton had a clear-cut job to do, because, while Carleton Whitney and those others like him would fire the shots, they wouldn't ever be the leaders. He had to ride to MF—which he didn't want to do because it was getting along towards summertime, the ride would be a hot one, and anyway, he couldn't believe talking to old Morton or Fisk would be too satisfactory.

Then Whitney raised his head, nodded at Fulton and walked away. He passed out of the saloon, swung southward and disappeared on down the sidewalk past the bar-room's broad window leaving Marshal Fulton still standing there loose and hip-shot with his fretful thoughts.

Several cowboys clattered past out in the sunlight and the mid-day stage from Tulsa rattled in, chain tugs dragging, horses sweat-shiny, dust in billows rising up from the wheels and a little bronzed monkey of a man perched high overhead tooling the vehicle on in.

Fulton sauntered out to stand in shade watching the stage brake down to a dusty halt and disgorge its passengers. There were two men in derby hats and pinstriped suits, each packing a large satchel. Drummers, those two; salesmen who made this southward swing twice a year taking orders from the mercantile establishments.

16

The third passenger was a girl of perhaps nineteen or twenty, high-breasted, wasp-waisted, with honey-yellow hair and large violet eyes. She held Fulton's attention longest because she was like a breath of fresh air to him; like a view of purest beauty after a long night's tossing. She watched the driver settle her bags in the dust, and just as Fulton started down to cross over and offer help, the last passenger alighted, and Fulton stopped because this one smiled down into the girl's upturned face, caught up her valise, and walked with her through the bright sunlight over to the hotel.

He wasn't tall and he wasn't particularly noticeable, that last stage passenger. In fact he looked the type to spend hours chewing idly upon a straw in front of a liverybarn watching people come and go.

Beneath the graceful curve of black hatbrim his face was boyish, freckled across the nose, and his mouth was too long and too lightly curving at its outer corners as though he were inwardly laughing at the world. His eyes were a slate grey colour and long dark lashes made them seem effeminate to Bob Fulton. He wasn't more than in his early twenties, but for all that he wore a walnut-stocked sixgun and it had a cut-away quick-draw holster and was held to his upper leg, not by the usual buckskin thong, but by a half-inch leather strap with a little fancy silver buckle, keeper, and tip.

17

Wearing a gun like that was an invitation, Fulton thought, and in this part of Oklahoma there were dozens of hard, rough men who would enjoy baiting a weedy kid out of nowhere; make him eat that damned little fancy tie-down.

Fulton was annoyed that the pretty girl had smiled up into the boy's face.

He walked back into Ab Slaughter's place a little soured by two annoyances in one morning, first that stupid Carleton Whitney, then that two-bit cowboy with his fancy gun.

Ab Slaughter was a man shaped like a beer barrel. He sloped inwards from waist to shoulders and from waist to knees. He was bald as a badger, wise as an owl, and rumour had it that Ab had quite a little money buried deep down in his sock. He had his opinions, had Ab, but mostly they were confined to politics; he ordinarily scorned the little brush-fire eruptions around the Ione country, but get Abner Slaughter started on what was wrong with the Territorial or Federal Governments, and he'd get as fired up as a switch-engine.

But today he was mellow, so, when Marshal Fulton came to rest against the bar Ab considered Bob's dour expression and said, 'Anythin' interesting come in on the stage?'

Fulton shrugged. 'A pretty girl, two drummers and a straw-haired cowboy with a fancy gun. Give me a beer, Ab.'

'You already had three straight shots this

18

morning, Bob.'

'Well dammit!'

'All right, all right.'

Ab got the beer, drew a second one, took them both back and kept one for himself. 'Sammy Holt the freighter said he seen another Texas drive comin' north when he was hauling in from over to Babbitt.'

Fulton was thinking of that lovely girl, wondering about her. She wasn't married to that string-bean cowboy because she hadn't been wearing a wedding ring. Still, riding a stage sometimes did things to people; you rode long enough and you got real friendly.

'Sammy said it looked like one of those crews old Colonel Bosworth sends out from the south Pecos country, Marshal.'

Fulton sipped his beer. What would a young, pretty girl like that be doing here in Ione, all alone? He put his empty glass down; he'd go find out. He had that right. After all, he was the law, and the law's business was to know things.

'What's the matter with you, Bob? You aren't even listening.'

Fulton swung, settled his gaze upon Ab and raised his eyebrows. 'You say something, Ab?'

'No,' snapped the stocky little saloon owner. 'Why would I say anything?' He turned and walked away with his shoulders pushed indignantly up and his back ramrod-straight.

Fulton watched Ab walk away thinking

Slaughter was sure getting edgy lately; couldn't even finish a beer before he got all indignant.

Fulton drained off Ab's beer too then sauntered on out into the morning sunlight again. He swung southward down towards the hotel; there was a springiness to his step which was not common. Also, there was a quick, sharp brightness to the marshal's dark eyes that was not customary either.

He turned in, crossed to the desk, flipped the register-book around and found a girl's name: Barbara Short. There were no other female names but underneath the name Barbara Short was a loose, heavy scrawl: Anthony Quayle. That, Fulton said to himself with distaste, would be the straw-thatched young cowboy.

CHAPTER THREE

'Well I could have told you as much,' boomed Big Jim Morton to the assembled cattlemen upon the porch of MF's main house after Carleton Whitney had glumly related his conversation with Marshal Fulton. 'Hell; the law simply don't care. Fulton's a shack-rat. Tell me the last time any of you've seen him outside town?'

No one answered, but then no answer was needed. Whitney sat there with his long legs

20

pushed out, with his coppery face sunk low, studiously considering the scuffed toes of his boots.

Buckley Fisk came out of the house with both hands full. He gave the door a hard kick and stepped forth with a bottle of whiskey in each hand. Without a word he handed the bottles around. While he was doing this he shot Big Jim a sly, upwards look. Jim was standing back; he slowly lowered and raised one eyelid. Then he boomed out heartily, saying, 'Drink up, boys. We're together in our determination, an' like I said day before yesterday—the hell with the law!'

Whitney took only a small swallow and passed the bottle along. He was the only man of the seven sitting or standing along Morton's and Fisk's front porch who didn't take a real pull. Then he dropped a bombshell, and his earlier reticence and scowling expression was explained.

'Before I left town I run into that half-Mex freighter who hauls in from Babbitt. Feller called Sammy something-or-other. You all have seen him around Ione.'

Someone wetly belched and muttered, 'Yeah; what about him?'

'He said he cut the sign of a Texas herd two days out of Ione comin' up the Panhandle trail.'

The whiskey bottles became still. All those faces turned, all those squinted eyes settled

21

upon Whitney. Big Jim Morton was the first to speak, but even Big Jim required a moment or two for digesting this alarming news.

'Two days out,' he said, 'and that was yesterday you seen the Mex freighter. That puts this new herd close to Ambush Canyon no later than tomorrow morning, if I'm figurin' right.'

'You are,' a thin-faced, greying older man said. 'In the canyon and through the pass by sometime tomorrow afternoon.'

'On our range,' put in Buckley Fisk. 'Did you say a *big* herd, Carleton?'

Whitney nodded. 'That's what I was told. One of them big Pecos herds. Maybe with six, eight riders along not counting the *cosinero* and the swamper.'

'Probably at least three thousand head,' murmured Jim Morton, turning to settle his big carcass upon a porch stringer that ran across from one overhang-post to another. 'Could even be more.'

A heretofore silent cattleman, a lanky, youthful-looking man with a dead cigarette dangling from his lips, looked straight up at Morton. 'At *least* three thousand head. More'n likely five, six thousand head. I tell you frankly, I'm runnin' short of grass for my own stock. If they camp and head for town like they always do, by gawd, boys, I can't put up with it. We been three springtime months now 'thout a drop of rain. If it don't come a rain directly,

22

why I tell you, that short-grass just ain't going to come back after it's once been grazed off.'

This man reached over, took one of the bottles, yanked the cork with his teeth, upended the thing and swallowed four times fast.

Whitney kept staring at his toes looking increasingly glum and long-faced. 'I tried to get Fulton to agree to ride out and warn 'em off. All he said was somethin' about fightin' a war, and then he mentioned land titles, and after that he stood there lookin' like he had a bellyache.'

'To hell with him,' exclaimed Buckley Fisk in his reedy, twanging voice. 'We don't need him anyway. All we need is for us seven, plus our riders, to be at this end of Ambush Canyon when that Texan point-rider comes through ahead of those cattle. That's all. You take about thirty, forty of us sitting there blockin' the trail, and no eight or nine cowboys in the world are going to start anything. They'll turn back and that'll be that.'

'I sure hope so,' said Carleton Whitney with quiet fervour. 'Jim; pass me that bottle, will you?'

Morton passed over the whiskey and said, 'The way I see it, we got to be there by sunup. That means me'n Buckley an' our men'll have to leave here tonight an' camp there; we got the farthest distance to travel, close to twenty miles. The rest of you, livin' north and

23

eastward anyhow, near the hills, can head out about five in the morning and meet us there after sunup.' Morton looked long and carefully at the seated men. 'That sound about right?' he asked.

They all nodded, even Whitney, so Big Jim had the answer he was after, which wasn't about when they should meet at all. He wanted to see them nod like that because it meant they were agreed and would be there come dawn, or shortly thereafter, and *that* was what Jim wanted to be sure of.

They spoke a little back and forth for an hour after that, mostly small-talk; about the lack of rain, range conditions, the price of beef delivered in Kansas City, Abilene and Dodge, but gradually their conversation petered out; they were soberly coming to think upon what might happen the following morning at the mouth of Ambush Canyon. Then they rose up and moved out to the hitchrack where their saddled animals were, and after muttering reassurances to one another that they'd be up there, come dawn or as soon thereafter as they could make it, *with* their riders, each man got astride and jogged on out of MF's yard.

Fisk returned to the shady porch, dropped down and took up one of the nearly emptied bottles. He tilted it, smacked his lips and put it down again watching Jim saunter on back too.

'Goin' to be some awful surprised Texas drovers, come morning,' Buckley said. 'Also

24

there just might be some badly surprised south-plains cattlemen. I got a feeling, Jim. If them cattle belong to old Bosworth from south of the Pecos, he don't hire any cowards.'

Morton jack-knifed into a chair too. He considered the whiskey bottles but didn't reach for one. He was sweating profusely, which was normal for Big Jim Morton, and he pushed his hat far back, but for as long as he could see those departing cattlemen he was quiet, his expression thoughtful. But afterwards, he hitched around in his chair and said, 'Buck; one thing we got to make damned clear to the riders. They're not to fire a single shot. Not even one. We got to impress that on 'em. When the fighting starts *they're not to shoot!*'

Fisk cleared his throat, spat over into a bed of weed-choked geraniums, and screwed up his face into a doubting expression. 'Don't know whether that'll work or not,' he opined. 'Pretty hard to keep fellers from firing back when someone's shooting at them.'

'I don't give a . . .' Big Jim gradually stiffened in his chair straining far out with his narrowed eyes. 'Who's that ridin' in from the east; can you make him out?'

Buckley straightened in his chair, watched the oncoming, distant rider for a long time, then said a mild oath. 'Yeah. It's the U.S. lawman from Ione. I wonder what *he* wants out here?'

'That damned Whitney,' growled Big Jim. 'I

25

figured he might shoot off his mouth an' get us involved with Fulton.'

'Maybe he didn't,' said Fisk, eyeing the oncoming horse and rider thoughtfully. 'Maybe Whitney didn't shoot off his mouth, Jim. Fulton's sure a long way from my idea of what a lawman should be, but I'll tell you one thing for damned sure—he ain't stupid. He's figured out for himself that if folks out this way are gettin' fired up about losing their grass every spring, we'd know about it.'

Big Jim reconsidered, picked up one of those bottles and tipped it. He afterwards replaced the cork, struck it roughly with one palm and put the bottle back down upon the porch floor. 'Let me handle this,' he said.

Fisk was already arising when Morton said this. He put a mild look down at his pardner and straightened up to his full height. 'I already had that in mind,' he said, and started down off the porch. 'I'll be out back at the corrals where the boys are brandin' those long-yearling colts.'

Big Jim was full of cordiality when Marshal Fulton came up and swung out of the saddle. He met the lawman at the foot of his porch and invited Fulton up into the shade, at the same time saying, 'Marshal, it's a mite warm for ridin' this time of year. You got something on your mind?' Big Jim was not only a man who seldom wasted words, he was also an almighty curious man.

26

Fulton said nothing until he was upon the porch and seated. He ran a slow look around MF's yard, saw dust rising out behind the big barn, also saw half a dozen cigarette stubs lying close by the porch, and those two nearly drained whiskey bottles. He could figure out the significance of these things without much trouble; the dust and noise from behind the barn didn't interest him but those bottles and smoked-down cigarette butts did. MF had recently had visitors. He regretted that he had not started out from Ione an hour earlier; he knew about who those visitors were and could imagine what they'd been over here discussing. If he could have also attended that meeting it would have saved him a lot of time and riding later.

'Talked to a neighbour of yours yesterday,' he finally told Morton. 'Carleton Whitney. He was upset about trail-herds grazing off the grass around here on their way north.'

'We're all a little worried about that,' said Big Jim, carefully giving the impression that *he* wasn't very worried. 'You got to understand Whitney's viewpoint, Marshal. Him and the others out here who don't have too much grass as it is, and are gettin' started, just naturally can't afford to be grazed over. Especially if this turns out to be a drought year. You got to understand it could break 'em.'

Fulton gazed down at the whiskey bottles. 'Kind of early in the day isn't it?' he mildly asked, giving Morton a chance to explain who'd been here helping him empty those bottles.

But Big Jim wasn't being drawn into anything. He chuckled and said, 'Sometimes morning's early for drinkin', and sometimes when a feller hasn't had none the night before, it's late for drinkin'. You care for a shot, Marshal?'

'No thanks,' answered Fulton, sounding unhappy about refusing. 'Jim; Whitney sounded like maybe the cattlemen out here might've been meeting; might've been getting fired up to do something about those trail-herds.'

'Did he, Marshal? Well now, you can't really blame 'em. Like I just told you—they can't afford to be eaten out every spring.' Morton's affability turned slightly barbed towards Fulton. 'They been tryin' to get someone to help 'em, but seems no one's very interested.'

Marshal Fulton put his dark gaze upon Morton and held it there. 'You'd know why *someone* hasn't helped them, wouldn't you, Jim?'

Morton's eyes became thin slits in his puckered face. 'I can imagine,' he murmured.

'I'll bet you can,' said Fulton dryly. 'It's a matter of land titles.'

'But them fellers got regular federal land patents. They were some of the first in the country to get full approval of ownership from

28

the government.'

'I know that, Jim. How about you? Have you and Buckley got approval on your claims yet?'

Morton spread his hands. 'We got a lawyer over in Guthrie workin' on it, Marshal. We'll get approval one of these days. After all, Fisk and I've been here a long time; longer'n anyone else. We were the real pioneers of this southwestern country, run off the redskins, hanged us a few rustlers, cleaned things up out here. The government'll come to see our claims are just and proper, in time. I'm not worryin'.'

'No,' drawled Bob Fulton, 'I don't think you are worrying, Jim. But that's not the point right now. The point is—long before those trail-herds hit Whitney's range, or the range of the other cattlemen, they cross about ten miles of MF land.'

'That's right,' agreed Big Jim smoothly. 'Eleven miles, to be exact.'

'And,' went on Fulton, 'if those northwesterly ranchers wanted to turn 'em back, the most logical place to do it would be at Ambush Canyon. Isn't that also right?'

'It is,' assented Morton, with a positive nod of his head.

'And, Jim, Ambush Canyon is at the easterly end of MF range. So, they'd be trying to turn the Texans back where they first hit MR. In other words, Jim, they'd be pulling your

29

chestnuts out of the fire by keeping the herds off MF's eleven miles of range.'

Morton looked over at Fulton full of geniality and quietly said, 'Well now, Marshal; that'd be one way of lookin' at it. But of course Buckley nor me see it quite like that. In fact we've been counsellin' the others to go slow; to give the law its chance to act first.' Morton's innuendo didn't escape Fulton. Big Jim was hinting that Fulton hadn't done his duty, hadn't offered to keep the peace. Then he said, 'But after all Buckley an' me, we got our own operation to worry about an' it's a full-time job, believe me, so about all we can do is talk to the others, from time to time.'

'Like this morning,' drawled Fulton, and Big Jim, who had been watching Fulton closely, knew he was referring to the whiskey bottles and cigarette stubs.

'A few rode over today, yes,' he said, and shrugged his thick shoulders.

'And they'd heard there was a herd on its way into the country.'

Big Jim rolled his shoulders again. 'Whitney picked up some such rumour in town yesterday, yes.'

Fulton pushed upright out of his chair, stepped to the porch edge, looked for a moment out over the springtime countryside, then turned and looked squarely at Big Jim Morton. 'Don't egg them on,' he said. 'If you do they'll be in hot water up to their ears.' He stepped down off the porch. '*Adios*, Jim; remember what I said.'

CHAPTER FOUR

Fulton didn't arrive back in town until well past midnight. He'd ridden north from MF to talk to Carleton Whitney and several of Whitney's nearest neighbours. It had been a fruitless ride because neither Whitney nor his friends were at home. They were out on the range somewhere branding and marking.

In fact, the entire arduous ride, so far as Fulton was concerned, was a total waste of time. That smiling hospitality of Morton's had rang as false with him as a lead coin, so, although he delivered a warning, he had no illusions about it being taken seriously.

Most of Ione was already abed as he came pacing down the roadway. There was a dwindling boisterousness at Ab Slaughter's place and a couple of the other local saloons, but generally, the town was quiet. He went out back and stabled his horse, forked him hay, poured a can of barley into his feed-box, hung up his outfit and trooped around to the roadside jailhouse door and entered. He was tired. There was a backdoor into the jailhouse but it was always kept locked and he didn't even feel like hunting in his pockets for the key. Besides, it wasn't much of a walk. The jailhouse was a converted barracks left over from army days. Actually, it had housed two married officers and their families, so it wasn't a very spacious building.

The lamp was burning inside. Since he hadn't been around to light it he wondered who had, and entered the front office with an expression of curiosity across his face.

Ab Slaughter was sitting there dozing. Across from Abner chewing a match, was that straw-thatched young stranger with the fancy gun-holster who had arrived in Ione the day before with that pretty little curvaceous girl with the violet eyes.

Fulton scarcely even nodded to the boy, although he was wide awake and smiled up at Fulton. He stepped over and shook Ab by the shoulder. 'Why aren't you up at the saloon or home in bed?' he asked, letting go the roused man's shirt and stepping over to his desk where he flung off his hat and sank down into a squeaky old swivel-chair. 'What's on your mind, Ab?'

Slaughter rubbed both eyes with fisted hands, cleared his throat meatily and jerked a stubby thumb at the straw-haired stranger. 'Him,' he replied. 'He's on my mind, Bob. You got to get him to leave town. I been talkin' to him like a Dutch uncle, but all he gives me is that boyish smile.' Slaughter ran his tongue around inside his mouth, walked over to the doorway and spat out into the night, walked back and sat down again. 'He whipped a man in my saloon tonight, Bob. Whipped an MF cowboy.'

Fulton drifted his dark stare around and met that smiling expression and those very clear, very blue eyes. He'd pegged this young stranger as a little rooster setting out in life to test his spurs, but now, gazing more closely at Anthony Quayle, he saw that this had been a mistake. There was something stirring in the depths of those boyish eyes that one did not ordinarily encounter in twenty- or twenty-one-year-old lads; something sly and old and knowing—something deadly.

The boy said, still wearing his soft smile, 'I'm Tony Quayle, Marshal.'

'Yeah I know. I saw your name on the hotel register yesterday right after you came in on the stage. What was the fight about up at Ab's place?'

'My fiancée, Marshal, Miss Barbara Short. That cowboy met her outside the hotel and said somethin' to her. She told me, so I went lookin' for him.'

'I see. What did he say?'

'That it sure was lonely at MF's bunkhouse and his bosses wouldn't care if she came out and stayed a spell.'

Fulton kept his close watch on Quayle as the lad talked. He detected the soft drawl of Texas right off, but it took a little longer for him to grudgingly concede that this boy wasn't really a boy at all. He was a man, and somewhere during his brief lifetime he'd learned all the ways of rough men, that boyish, clear-eyed look and soft smile notwithstanding.

He sighed and faced Ab. 'Sounds like he was justified; that is, if it happened like he just told me.'

Ab frowned disapprovingly. 'It might have. I don't know about that, Bob. Leastways I expect it *does* get lonesome at MF. But that ain't the point.' Ab jabbed at Quayle with his stubby thumb. 'It's the way he fought that don't set well with me. He come up behind that MF cowboy, tapped him on the shoulder, an' when the feller turned, he hit him so hard he went half across the room, busted two chairs and a table. Then he lit into him like a wildman. He had that cowboy leaking blood from the nose, the mouth, and one busted ear before we could haul him off. He'd have killed the danged fool, Bob.' Ab paused, glared, and drew in a big, indignant breath. 'There was three other MF men in there an' they'd have gunned Quayle then an' there, if I hadn't thrown down on 'em with my riot-gun from behind the bar. Now; you got to talk some sense into him; I been tryin' half the night an' all I get is that silly smile. He won't leave town.'

Fulton thought he had the picture now, so

34

he faced back towards the straw-haired youth. 'Mister Slaughter's right,' he said quietly. 'MF's a bad outfit to tangle with. There are about ten riders, and the owners, Fisk and Morton, are noted for standin' solidly behind their men.'

Young Quayle said, 'Thanks for the interest, Marshal, but unless you figure to lock me up, why I reckon I'll drift on over to the hotel and get some sleep.' He stood up. He wasn't quite six feet tall but a natural lean litheness made him appear taller. 'I agreed to sit around here waitin' for you to ride in, an' I've kept my word on that. But I'm not leavin' Ione; at least not unless you want to run me out.'

Fulton leaned back studying young Quayle. This one wasn't the kind you could talk to, he decided, and made one last feeble effort, not because he liked what he saw—he didn't—but because he was wistfully thinking of that lovely girl over at the hotel.

'Quayle; this is a rough town and a rough country. If you're going to go around jumpin' every woman-starved trailhand who looks at Miss Barbara, then you're going to be pretty damned busy. Take my advice; relax. Be a little tolerant and understanding. I know how you feel; believe it or not I was your age once. I used to walk around with my spurs let out a notch so's they'd ring when I went past. But I was lucky. I grew up where folks were a little more civilised. Otherwise I suppose I'd have

35

been killed long ago. Don't you make the same mistakes.'

The lad's eyes never left Fulton's face all through this little sermon. They were respectful and attentive, but they were also like wet iron. When Fulton finished Quayle stepped to the door, lay a hand upon the latch and said, 'Thanks for the advice, Mister Fulton. Good night.' He passed out of the office, gently eased the door closed, and Ab Slaughter mumbled a mild curse.

'Danged Texans,' he said over at Fulton. 'You know what I think? I think when everyone else in America is civilised, Texans'll still be swaggerin' around carryin' guns and darin' anyone to say they aren't the roughest, toughest, hardest-drinkin', hardest-ridin' folks in the wide world.'

'They've had reason to get like that,' yawned Fulton. 'It's been a bloody business for them, just stayin' alive.'

Slaughter stood up, scratched his head and paced over to the door waggling his head and scowling. 'You should've seen that young mountain lion, Bob. Why, he went after that MF man like they'd been mortal enemies from birth.'

'Maybe in a way they have been, Ab. One thing you've got to hand Texans—they don't believe in off-colour talk around womenfolk. Maybe more of us ought to be a little like that at times.'

36

'Hell,' growled Slaughter, glaring. 'You're turning into a philosopher, and that's *one* thing we don't need in Oklahoma Territory.'

Fulton stood up smiling, his dark handsome face lined with fatigue. 'Go close up,' he said, opening the door for his visitor, then he stood there with his smile beginning to fade. 'What the hell's that kid doing here anyway, and whoever heard of a cowboy taking a room at the hotel for more than one night?'

'I don't know. I don't even care. From now it's your headache, Bob. But I'll tell you one thing; the next time MF hits town they'll be lookin' for that yellow-haired cock-of-the-walk, and when the smoke clears away you'll be picking him up in a dustpan.'

Slaughter departed. Fulton closed the door after him and stood a long moment with his hand resting upon the latch. He said aloud, 'I wouldn't bet on that, Ab. I wouldn't bet on it. I'm beginning to get a feeling that Anthony Quayle isn't quite the puppy he looks like.'

There wasn't much to do after Slaughter's departure in the way of closing up for the night. Fulton had no prisoners—hadn't had since one of Carleton Whitney's three cowboys had been jugged ten days earlier for being drunk and disorderly—so he checked the doors, blew out the lamp, walked out into the night-hushed roadway, looked left and right, saw and heard nothing, and started on over to the room he hired by the month at Ione's only hotel.

At the lobby the night-clerk nodded sleepily as Fulton headed for the stair casing and started up. Upon the landing where he halted to fish around for his key it was gloomy from one overhead hanging lamp which hadn't had its wick trimmed in a month and was odorously smoking. He found the key, inserted it, then hesitated at the soft sound of voices coming from on down the gloomy hall.

He recognised the masculine voice at once because not more than twenty minutes before he'd been listening to it over at the jailhouse. The other voice, softer, more musical, had to belong to the lovely little girl, Barbara Short.

Fulton stood a moment running this matter through his mind, and finally he turned, passed softly down to the doorway beyond which those voices were coming, and briefly listened, then rapped.

The voices were instantly silent. Fulton rapped again. The door opened with young Quayle filling it. He had his right hand within inches of that strapped-down gun he wore.

Fulton said mildly, 'Pretty late; maybe you'd better go along to your own room and bed down.'

Quayle's blue gaze gradually hardened. He considered Fulton for several quiet seconds before he said in a thin-edged, soft drawl, 'This here is quite a town, Marshal. I never had folks take such an interest in seeing that I get protected before. And that I get plenty of rest.'

Fulton gazed into that boyish face beginning to strongly dislike Anthony Quayle. 'All right,' he said evenly. 'Let me put it another way. This is also a respectable town, Tony, and fiancée or not, it isn't going to do either of you any good being in that hotel room together this late at night.'

'Marshal . . . !'

Fulton waited, seeing the slow rise of dark blood into Quayle's face. He braced into it saying nothing, but ready.

From beyond sight of the doorway the girl said, 'Good night, Tony. I'll meet you for breakfast.'

Fulton wished he could have seen her face when she said that because it was a very wise thing to say right then and he wanted to see whether she was actually that wise, or just happened to say the right thing at the right time.

Then she came up behind young Quayle and Fulton had his answer. She had her wealth of wavy taffy-blonde hair let down. It fell across her shoulders like spun gold. She didn't quite come up to Quayle's shoulder, but up close she was in Fulton's eyes even more beautiful than she'd looked the day before. And he also had his answer. Her eyes were rock-steady and knowing as she brushed Quayle's right arm with a light touch.

'Good night—both of you,' she murmured, and smiled.

The tension was broken. Fulton smiled back. Young Quayle lost his stiffness. He turned, looked into her eyes, stepped through and closed the door.

Fulton felt that little pang of regret again as he turned away, and it made him feel a lot less antagonistic towards the younger man. As they moved along down the corridor he tried once more to get past Tony Quayle's veiled reserve.

'I reckon you've got me pegged for a meddler. Well; it sure looks that way, I've got to admit. But back there, all I was trying to do was get across to you that in this country, it doesn't take much to start tongues wagging, and since I know you don't like loose talk, I thought maybe we could prevent that.'

Quayle stopped before a door and said sardonically, 'At one o'clock in the morning, Marshal?'

'At one o'clock in the morning, Tony. These walls have ears. For instance, I've got the room three doors west, but even that far off I heard you two talking in there.' Fulton waved towards all the other closed doors. 'There are folks in nearly every room. I expect they're asleep by now, but I sure wouldn't bet on it.'

Quayle opened his door, turned and gazed straight out at Fulton. He seemed about to speak, but in the end he only nodded, passed on inside and closed the door.

40

Fulton moved on down to his own room, let himself in and lit a table-lamp. He gazed at himself briefly in the mirror, made a wry face and began unbuckling his shell-belt. Once, in Arizona Territory there had been a girl like Barbara Short. She'd been taller, maybe not so well put together, but she'd had the same taffy-coloured hair and the same violet eyes.

But four years was a long time. He hadn't heard from her in three years now, which had its significant meaning, but that didn't stop a man from quietly remembering either.

Fulton got into bed with a composite of faces haunting him: Big Jim Morton's slyly smiling face, young Tony Quayle's unsmiling face, Barbara's soft-smiling features, and finally, the troubled face of Carleton Whitney.

CHAPTER FIVE

The country around Ione was level to rolling with bois d'arc, scrub-oak, and redbud trees scattered across it. In a good year the grass, which never seemed to stand more than six inches off the ground, had a nutritional value that was truly startling. Within thirty days after the last frost, horses, cattle, even deer, who are not ordinarily so much grazing animals as they are browsing animals, were greasy fat.

But it took rain to maintain this abundant

natural resource; without rain the graze turned brown early in the year, and this particular spring the rain was overdue.

Northward stood the low flint hills with dark folds where trees grew. Beyond these soft-rounded lifts stood higher hills, darker still, with more forestation and underbrush. The highest of those northwesterly peaks marked the age-old raider-route where wild Comanches had passed along on their way up out of Texas' Panhandle country and Staked Plains, but that had been some time ago, and now the only riders who traced out the ancient route were drovers on their way through Oklahoma towards the Great Plains of Kansas and Nebraska, where the booming post-war cattle markets were.

It was towards that highest pass that Marshal Fulton rode with morning's soft pink light around him, for that particular high pass was Ambush Canyon, so named because once, long past, Ranald McKenzie's Regulars had ambushed a big raiding party of Quanah Parker's Comanches here, had decimated the red marauders, and had broken the back of resistance to the White Tide.

But Ambush Canyon was a drowsy place now, so many years later, with its quiet shadows, its groves of trees, and its well-worn old meandering trail which passed for two miles through short-grass toward the westerly debouchment where MF range began.

Fulton wanted to satisfy himself about that rumour of a Texas herd on the move, but also, he wanted to see whether or not the cattlemen were also up there to seek the same confirmation, and if they were, he had something to say to them.

It was pleasant, riding around those first rolling hills. It was still too early for the daytime heat to begin building. Morning's softness lay like a benediction making the land good, and also making it soft to the eyes which it would not be after the heat came to reflect off every polished stone surface with a hard glitter.

Fulton rode along with his private thoughts, as men without families or ties often do, interested in the threads of other men's lives, not only because it was his job to know things, to figure them out, but also because his own social existence was a blank. There were women in Ione exactly as there was also a proportionate number of men, but in Fulton's circle of acquaintance he'd met few indeed he cared much about. Even among the men, outside of Ab Slaughter and perhaps one or two others, Fulton had no close friends.

It didn't bother him; he wasn't exactly a 'loner' but neither was he a socialising man. He took his work seriously and it absorbed most of his time. There were little moments, like the night before when Barbara Short reminded him of someone, when he felt wistful, felt that life was hurrying on past, but because Fulton was not the brooding type, he seldom dwelt upon something which was past and painful.

He was a quiet, steady type man with a strong streak of fatalism in him. He sometimes appeared to have Indian ways; he could gaze straight at a man for sixty seconds without moving or saying a word, but he could also turn violent in a twinkling, for Bob Fulton hadn't come by his dark good looks accidentally. His grandmother *had* been Indian.

There was a cool shade upon the south slope of Ambush Canyon. He passed into it and out of it following a little angling game trail always upwards. He came across a slight depression where, for some obscure reason, prairie dogs had built an extensive village. He was very careful here; many a good horse had broken a leg falling through one of these underground mazes. Beyond the prairie dog settlement the trail swung down into a narrow place and there Fulton found a tiny spring with its clear-water pool. He allowed his horse to drink and pushed along again. The crest of this south slope was less than a quarter mile onward. If it seemed that Fulton had taken the hard way to find out whether there were drovers in the canyon, a little reflection would have pointed out that by making for the ridge he'd be able to not only see a long way eastward through Ambush Canyon, he'd also be high enough to command an excellent view of the westerly country too, which was where the cattlemen would be, if they were up here at all.

And they were. He saw them almost the moment he topped out upon his gravelly rim. It looked as though there were at least thirty of them. Distance and altitude prevented him from making any positive identifications, but there was no mistaking their purpose in being fanned out across the mouth of Ambush Canyon like that, some squatting in the soft sunlight, some sauntering along that long line stopping now and then to talk. They were there to do exactly what Fulton had thought they might do—stop a trail-drive.

He looked off eastward. It was a little like being a spectator at something one had no hand in, for more than a mile off he spotted two riders coming along side by side down the canyon, riding slouched and easy as point-riders usually ride, and farther back a good long mile, was the dust and noise and red-moving tide of hundreds of cattle.

Fulton looped his reins, tipped back his hat and had a saturnine thought. Why was it that men bound for trouble always spoilt the most lovely time of day with their anger and their violence?

He watched for a while, satisfied the Ione-country cowmen had no riders on up the canyon scouting, and decided that since he knew those local men he could deal with them later, that right now the thing for him to do was halt those Texans where they were—a goodly distance out of gun range of the waiting men out on MF's range. He sighed, took up his reins and swung eastward to pass along as far as the first worthwhile downwards trail. There, with the saddle cantle gouging him from behind, he allowed his animal to pick its own way down into the shade and gloomy solitude of Ambush Canyon.

He touched flat country a half hour later, saw the point-riders slogging along and eased out of some trees directly into their path. Both those Texans saw him at once and drew sharply, alertly upright in their saddles. He saw them swiftly speak back and forth, but they neither reined up nor slowed their advance.

They were both young men in their early twenties. They were dusty, unshaven, armed with booted carbines and belt-guns. Each carried the rawhide *riata* of Mexican-Texas and rode with the slightly crooked knees—called *la jinetta* by Mexicans—which was typical of the brush-country where they'd obviously originated. They were lean, long men with the startlingly white foreheads of men who'd been riding a long time into the sun with hats tugged low, but otherwise their faces were nearly copper coloured, and now, their faces were also carefully smoothed out and intently

46

watchful.

When they were close enough Fulton reined up and let them pass over that last hundred yards towards him. He nodded gravely.

'I'm U.S. Marshal Bob Fulton from Ione, which is south of here, and I'd like a few words with your boss.'

One of the youthful Texans said in a soft drawl, 'I'm Fred Whorton and this here's my pardner, Joel Dunlap. The trail-boss is a couple miles back. He'll talk to you, Marshal, but the owner's gone on into Ione to see some folks.'

Fulton said, 'All right. What's the trail-boss's name?'

'Hudson Marsh. He's a West Texas man.'

Fulton came near to smiling. Whorton had said this Hudson Marsh was a 'West Texas man' as though that made Marsh a special breed of person; as though there were only Texans in this world and *West* Texans were something superior to ordinary Texans. He said, 'Let's ride back and hunt him up.'

The second rangerider, the one named Joel Dunlap, spoke up finally, saying, 'You ride on back, Marshal, but we got to keep pointin' the way.'

Fulton shook his head at Dunlap. 'That won't be necessary because the herd stops right where it is. I think if you two ride back with me you can help hold it when we meet the other riders.'

47

'Stop?' said Dunlap, regarding Fulton steadily. 'What for, Marshal? We figured to be ten miles past this here canyon before quittin' time today.'

'You can forget making that ten miles,' said Fulton, and took up his rein hand. 'Just beyond the mouth of this pass, out where the range begins again, are something like thirty armed cattlemen waiting to stop you.'

Dunlap's jaw went slack. He looked from Fulton to Fred Whorton and back to Fulton again, but he didn't say anything. Whorton was also surprised, but he showed it less and recovered quicker. He abruptly turned his horse; there were splotches of angry colour in his tanned cheeks. 'Come along then,' he said, and booted out his mount into a lope.

Fulton rocketed along with these two until the taste of trailherd-dust was strong in the roiled air and he made out three more riders moving along with the first wave of wicked-horned cattle. He slowed to allow Dunlap and Whorton to whip on ahead and explain to those other men. Then, when he came on up they knew, and regarded him stonily. Whorton spun away racing down the side of those plodding-along cattle. Where the animals began piling up behind Dunlap and the others, there was a sharp little sound of clicking horns, and later, bawling protest at being crowded upon by the rearward animals.

The Texans said nothing as Fulton came up,

halted, and considered them almost stoically. He knew the breed well; they were bad men to cross and right now they were beginning to feel crossed. They swore a little at the pushing cattle and flagged with hats to hold them back, they sashayed their spade-bit horses with one finger, catching a bolter here and there before he'd gotten his speed up. They were efficient men at their trade, top trailhands obviously, and this meant to Marshal Fulton that they'd hurrahed their share of cow towns—and cow-town marshals. Although these Texas men, like every other breed of people upon the face of this earth, came in endless variety individually, they nevertheless had one trait in common. They made the best friends a man could hope for and they also made the best enemies he could hope not to have.

After a while Whorton came racing back. He had a greying, grizzled, blocky, bull-like shorter and older man with him, and the moment this man speared Fulton with his perpetually squinted hard bright eyes, Fulton knew he was gazing at Hudson Marsh.

Whorton jerked his head at Fulton saying simply, 'That's him, Hud.'

Marsh eased his mount on over and barely nodded. Without a wasted word he said, 'What's this all about, Marshal?'

Fulton completed his appraisal of the shorter, older man while he was replying. 'The local cattlemen mean to turn you back, Mister

Marsh. They're fearful of a drought-year and if you trail over their ranges and camp, your critters'll eat off the ground-cover.'

Marsh had a lipless slash of a mouth, a massive blunt, square jaw, and the sum total of his powerful, squatty appearance added up to just one thing: determination.

He said: 'Marshal; why do you figure we pushed up the trail so early this year? Because Texas is dry too an' you can't sell bones with a taut hide stretched over 'em up on the Kansas plains. We got no choice but to keep going. As for not crossing—maybe the owner'll be willing to pay passage, I don't know. I can't speak for him an' he rode on down to Ione before sunup this morning. But we got to move the herd out of this canyon; we can't hold 'em here without water for long.'

'Then I think you'd better turn back, Mister Marsh, where there *is* water.'

'Turn back!' exclaimed the Texan, showing brusque anger. 'Marshal; it's a day's drive back to water.'

'Mister Marsh,' said Fulton quietly, giving the angry trail-boss look for look, 'if you *don't* turn back—if you let these cattle bust past an' get onto the range beyond—you're going to be responsible for trouble. You see, there are something like thirty or thirty-five armed cattlemen out there waiting for you, blocking off the mouth of this canyon.'

Hudson Marsh's knuckles whitened around

his reins. He swung to gaze over where Whorton, Dunlap, and those other three riders were sitting discreetly apart from this exchange. From time to time one of these men would flag back a crowding-up critter but otherwise they were closely and intently watching Fulton and their trail-boss.

Marsh squared back around. Fulton read his expression correctly and braced into the wrath that emanated from Marsh. 'Listen, Marshal; going back's out of the question. We're two days behind schedule as it is because of swollen rivers. We got no choice but to try an' reason with them cattlemen beyond the pass. If you like you can come with me, but we can't hold 'em here very long—we got to go ahead.'

Fulton had anticipated something like this—some kind of an attempt at compromise—and he thought it might possibly work, providing Jim Morton and Buckley Fisk were not out there with Whitney and the others, so he nodded at Marsh, saying, 'Warn your men not to let a single critter get past, Mister Marsh, and we'll go have a talk beyond the canyon.'

Marsh bawled angry orders over his shoulder, urged out his animal and went along beside Marshal Fulton, his granite jaw set solidly, resolutely, towards the distant break in the hilly skyline.

Fulton rode in silence. Sometimes an affair like this ended simply; sometimes it did not.

51

Only the Lord knew how this one would end, and He wasn't saying.

CHAPTER SIX

The moment Marshal Fulton came out of Ambush Canyon with Hudson Marsh at his side, he knew there would be no compromise. Sitting their horses a hundred yards ahead with all ten of their riders strung out behind them, were both Big Jim Morton and Buckley Fisk, and for once Big Jim wasn't wearing any mask of false geniality; he was looking straight ahead with a flintiness upon his heavy features which could be read by Fulton even at that considerable distance.

Marsh, looking a little surprised at all those men lined up across the canyon's mouth although he'd been informed about how many to expect, said, 'Which one do we talk to?'

Fulton didn't reply, he simply reined toward Morton and Fisk. But just before they came within hearing distance he said, 'Mister Marsh; don't start anything. The only thing getting mad will do is make damned certain you don't go through at all.'

Marsh was studying those two over there on their saddle horses and did not reply. When he and Marshal Fulton came up and halted though, Hudson Marsh solemnly nodded.

52

Morton nodded back but Buckley didn't; Buckley sat up there like a carved statue of a man, his deaths-head, taut-skinned face totally without expression except up around the eyes; there, Buckley looked unrelenting and ready.

'Didn't expect to see you, Marshal,' said Big Jim, with none of his usual booming heartiness; with resentment showing in his veiled and hooded eyes.

'I'm not always leaning on Ab Slaughter's bar,' said Fulton dryly, then turned brisk. 'Mister Marsh here is trail-boss for that herd you were told was coming along. He's holding up back in the canyon, but he can't hold 'em forever in there and he'd like to discuss at least coming out this far and camping until something else can be worked out. He could drift his cattle up north to Copperhead Creek for water, and bring them back.'

Buckley Fisk began negatively shaking his head before Fulton was half through speaking, but he never once glanced at the marshal, he kept staring straight over at Hudson Marsh.

Other cattlemen began drifting up, some astride, some walking along leading their animal. Carleton Whitney was one of the first to halt and look around as he listened. The others though were not far behind. Before the last man was up, all but five or six indifferent cowboys sitting crossed legged back northward a short distance smoking and gossiping, were there, and every man was scrupulously

53

attentive without speaking or even seeming to wish to speak.

'It's no good like that,' said Buckley to Fulton. 'There ain't no half way method of doin' things, Marshal. You either turn 'em back or you don't. He either stays in that canyon or he comes out and spreads all over our range.' Fisk looked Hudson Marsh straight in the eye. 'How many head you drivin'?' he asked.

Marsh answered promptly and candidly. 'Forty-five hundred head, all trail-branded so they won't get mixed into anybody's herd.'

Fulton, watching Fisk, felt irritated at the adamant stand Big Jim's pardner was taking. He said: 'Jim; I thought you told me yesterday you advised these neighbours to take it easy in this.'

Two dozen heads lifted and two dozen sets of eyes swerved to linger upon Big Jim's oily face. But Morton was equal to the occasion by employing innuendo. 'Marshal; I also told you since the law don't do nothin' for local cattlemen they'd maybe have to do something for themselves, an' after all, Buckley and I are local cattlemen. Our interests lie with our neighbours. We got to protect our grass too.'

Fulton looked past, saw one MF rider with a pulpy, swollen face and a bandaged mouth, looked past this one to all the others and dryly said, 'Jim; the only man missing from your crew is the cook. Why didn't you bring him along too? For a man with peaceful instincts you're sure out here this morning loaded for bear.'

Big Jim made his greasy smile at Fulton, but the eyes weren't smiling. 'Well now, Marshal,' he exclaimed. 'How'd we know what these here drovers might try to do? After all, a man'd be a plain idiot to head into maybe eight, ten of these trail-drovers without a little backing, wouldn't he?'

Hudson Marsh said in a brittle tone, 'Mister; we're not troublesome men. That is, not unless we got to be. Then we try to give as good as we get. It's all right with me the whole passel of you showed up here. Maybe it's best this way; everybody knows what's said. All I'm asking is that you let us come out of that canyon and hold the herd here, near water, until somethin' can be worked out between the owner and you boys.'

'Where is the owner?' Morton asked.

'In Ione. He rode in right early this morning. But I'll send a man after him the second I get back to the herd. Like I told Marshal Fulton; maybe he'll agree to pay passage. We've had to do that before. But I can't definitely say that he will. That's for him to say.'

Buckley Fisk parted his lips to speak but Carleton Whitney spoke up first. He wasn't looking at Fisk, didn't know Fisk had been about to also speak. Whitney said, 'They got a

55

problem, Jim. Marsh's right; unless he goes ten miles back there's no water, and without that, he can't hold forty-five hundred head in the canyon, even if he had an army of men with him.'

'How many riders you got?' asked Big Jim.

'Eleven, counting myself,' replied Marsh. 'Not nearly enough to do what you're asking, Mister Morton.'

'We'll loan you another ten,' said Buckley Fisk. He glanced around at the others. 'I say he can stay in the canyon or he can go ten miles back—it's all the same to me.'

Fulton put a smouldering glance over at Fisk. 'It'd help matters, Buck, if you'd be reasonable,' he quietly said, controlling the rising anger within him.

Fisk snarled back: 'Marshal; you taking sides? I thought your job was to be neutral; at least to protect the folks who're payin' your wages.'

Fulton's face got steadily darker as he and Buckley Fisk glared across the intervening distance. Big Jim spoke up again, saying with mild reproach, 'Easy, boys, easy. We got a problem here. Gettin' mad won't help anythin'. Tell me, Mister Marsh; would the owner pay a reasonable fee for campin' right here until we can settle this—and give his word he won't head out in the night across our ranges?'

Hudson Marsh was in a corner and it

showed. He said, choosing his words with great care, 'Mister Morton; I think he'd do that. But like I already said, I can't speak for him. Only I feel he'll agree to that.'

'Well now,' said Big Jim slyly. 'It'd sure be better'n trailing back ten miles wouldn't it? If he's a reasonable man he'd sure know that, wouldn't he?'

'Yes, he'd know that.'

'Well then, since this is MF range an' Mister Fisk and I control MF range, I expect the fee'll be up to us.'

Fulton began to get the drift of this as he watched Big Jim turn and gaze mildly at Buckley Fisk. They were going to hold the Texans up. He tried to head this off but didn't bring it off. He said, speaking swiftly, 'The usual rate is around a nickel a head, I think.'

Big Jim's face mirrored reproof at this. 'Marshal,' he said, sounding pained. 'Your work is keepin' the peace. Ours is beef, an' for a nickel a head we'll keep the grass because it'll net us at least a dime, while once these here Texas cattle have grazed it down to the dust, it'll cost us five times that to get it back again. No, Marshal; I figure we should have at least two bits a head.'

Marsh sat there looking at Big Jim, his eyes turning hard and baleful. But he was a man of strong control, for when next he spoke his voice was as mild as it could be.

'That's mighty high, Mister Morton, mighty

high. For two bits a head we could cross the planted farmer-fields of eastern Oklahoma.'

'That's your privilege, Mister Marsh,' said Big Jim smoothly. 'In fact I sort of wonder why all you Texas drovers don't do that. You could be puttin' on tallow while you're on the way to market.'

Marsh sat there rapidly thinking, rapidly calculating. As Fulton watched, he saw the granite-jawed Texan's cheeks brighten to a rosy red and his pale eyes dance dangerously. Finally, with all those men watching him closely, Marsh said, 'I want you to understand I can't make this final. I'm only trail-boss. But I think the owner'll agree to it. At least I'll sure try to get him to.'

Big Jim struck his saddlehorn with a massive fist. 'Done,' he exclaimed in his booming voice. 'Now what we got to work out is a meetin' between us fellers and your boss.'

'That'll be no problem,' said Marsh dryly, 'he'll be in town the rest of today and maybe tomorrow too. You can see him there. I'll have a rider tell him to meet you at Marshal Fulton's office tomorrow morning bright an' early.'

'Not too early,' said Big Jim, genially smiling. 'It's a seventeen mile ride from MF to Ione.' He chuckled and waved an expansive hand. 'I was only jokin' Mister Marsh; we'll be there.'

Marsh gave everyone but Buckley Fisk a

brittle little nod and reined around. Fulton hesitated a moment, then also turned. He'd decided that since Morton had gotten his way there would be no trouble from that direction, but Marsh was mad clear through and since he didn't know any of these Texans he thought he'd ride back a ways at least, with their trail-boss.

They were entering the canyon before Hudson Marsh swung from the waist, said Big Jim's name, added a sizzling oath to it, and exclaimed: 'Seven hundred and twenty-five dollars, Marshal. That's plain out'n out highway robbery, an' I think if a U.S. lawman hadn't been sittin' right there I'd have told that mountain of lard to go straight to hell!'

'If you had, Mister Marsh, you'd have had to turn your herd around and drive it back ten miles, then spend a week finding a fresh way through the country—*if* you were lucky. If you *weren't* lucky . . .' Fulton lifted his shoulders and dropped them. 'Men have been buried hereabouts for a whole lot less.'

'Seven hundred and twenty-five dollars,' repeated the burly, greying Texan. 'Why hell; that's near as much as the wages we pay good Texas trailhands from the Pecos to the Kansas plains. And Marshal; I got my doubts about the owner paying it. I'll keep any end of the bargain; I'll talk up to him like a Mormon deacon to get agreement, but even if he does pay you're goin' to be able to hear him cuss from here to the Rio Grande.'

They got back where the bawling of cattle, the dust and loud profanity of eight sweat-drenched men and horses were fighting a grim battle, and there it was no longer possible to talk because of the noise. Fulton pulled off to one side. Marsh loped on over and shouted instructions, then, as his red-faced riders began to break up, to take their trailing positions again as the herd started onward towards the grassy plains beyond, Hudson Marsh returned to his position beside Marshal Fulton, spat dust, and asked about Copperhead Creek. By then the herd was streaming past, crowding those two up the rearward slope.

'About a mile and a half due north from the mouth of this canyon,' loudly replied Fulton. 'You'll see creekwillows long before you see the water. This time of year there'll be ample water; later on it dries down to a trickle.'

Marsh nodded impatiently, then said, 'Marshal; I'm obliged to you. If I can get away I'll come on into town in the morning and sit in on that meeting. One thing's danged sure— I got to see the boss before Morton springs that seven hundred dollar fee on him, or he'll explode right in Morton's face.'

Fulton waved his hand and turned to head on up the slope back the way he'd gotten down here. He didn't particularly want to do this, it was needlessly hard on his horse, but he didn't cherish the idea of sitting through this acrid dust until forty-five hundred cattle went past either.

He was part way up letting his horse blow a moment before resuming his way, when he distantly made out the chuckwagon far back in the dusty drag, and a second high-wheeled old battered vehicle, also drawn by four tough little mules, which was the 'possible' wagon; the rig which was used for hauling bedrolls, warbags, extra clothing, extra ammunition, everything it was possible to get in there which could neither be carried behind a rider's saddle or put into the chuckwagon.

He was watching that drag before resuming his way when something caught his eye. Very few rangeriders ever owned white shirts, and even the ones who did never wore them except at weddings or funerals. But the driver of that 'possible' wagon was wearing one. Not only that, the driver was also sitting up there in all that gritty dust without his neckerchief up over nose and mouth.

Fulton looked and wondered, then shook his head and urged his horse out again. He went along almost to the top-out before halting for another brief 'blow', and cast another look outward and downward.

Now, the cattle were on up through the canyon, the drag was directly below, and that 'possible' wagon was directly in his low-down line of vision. Fulton got his biggest shock of the day then; that wasn't a man driving those four mules, it was a *woman*! Not only that, it wasn't a very old woman either, because she looked straight up as Fulton was looking straight down, and where the soft sunlight cut through strong-smelling dust, she looked young, perhaps twenty years of age, certainly no older, and she was quite handsome.

Fulton sat there watching until the wagons were past and lurching on down the canyon. This was the first time in his life he'd ever heard of an owner fetching along his wife on a trail-drive. He gigged his horse, made the crest, cast a final look downward and solemnly told himself that if there was one thing about Texans a person could be sure of, it was their uninhibited unpredictability. Then he set his course straight for town.

CHAPTER SEVEN

Ab Slaughter strolled over where Marshal Fulton leaned upon the bar sipping beer, and surveyed the lawman's dusty clothing. There was a cloying scent that made Ab wrinkle his nose.

'You been around cattle,' Ab said. 'What you need is a bath.'

Fulton eyed Slaughter over the rim of his glass, drank, set the glass aside and said, 'What

I need is ten deputies and the luck of the Irish. Yeah, I've been with cattle, Ab. Rode out and had a look at that Texas herd north of town at Ambush Canyon.'

'Big herd?'

'Forty-five hundred head. Fill the glass again.'

Slaughter dutifully went along to draw off another beer. As he'd done before, Ab also drew off a glass for himself. When he returned and set Fulton's glass upon the bartop he said, 'There's a rumour floating around town that MF and the westerly cattlemen are goin' to turn that herd back.'

Fulton held his refilled glass without lifting it. 'Did it ever strike you odd, how often rumours have a lot of truth in them, Ab?'

Slaughter shrewdly watched Fulton's face for a moment. 'So they *are* going to try it,' he said. 'Now I'm beginnin' to understand what you been up to all day.'

There was a soft-saffron glow off in the distant west which cast its long, mellow light down across Ione, and some of that light struck through Slaughter's roadside window to colour-in the saloon's interior.

There was a sifting of townsmen and rangeriders in the place. The latter mostly hung around Ab's free-lunch counter making beef and onion sandwiches, while the townsmen stood quietly along the bar taking a moment's respite with a beer or a slug of rye whiskey before heading on home after the end of Ione's business day.

It was a peaceful setting; one that appealed to Bob Fulton because of its warm, quiet lassitude. He hooked one spurred boot over the brass rail, leaned with both elbows upon the bar and steadily regarded little Ab Slaughter.

'Funny thing about people, Ab. The more they have the more they seem to want.' Fulton was thinking of Buckley Fisk and Big Jim Morton. 'You'd figure when men've been a quarter century getting somewhere, they'd slack off when the goal was reached. But no; I think what happens is that ambition becomes a habit. I think rich men'd up and die if they quit trying to be richer. All the juice would be squeezed out of life for them. Their purpose for existing would be gone, and they'd die. And they know this, Ab, so they go on striving.'

Ab said, 'Quite a philosophy, Marshal. Let me add something to it.' Ab sipped, put down his glass and looked straight at Fulton, his eyes narrowed in a shrewd, knowing way. He understood perfectly who Fulton was thinking of without the marshal even giving him a hint. 'Let's say a man makes his money and achieves his success when things are a lot different; when they're more raw and violent and lawless. Well now; he learns certain tricks under those conditions which he still employs

64

twenty-five years later, when conditions have changed, and maybe hangin' suspected rustlers and puttin' a cocked .45 to an Indian's head worked in those early days, but all of a sudden it's illegal to do those things. So, the rich man winds up in a peck of bad trouble.'

Fulton's eyes softened towards little Ab. He almost smiled. 'I reckon we understand who this man might be, don't we, Ab?'

'We understand, Marshal. There are a lot of folks in town who understand. Only it's not one man, it's two men.'

'Yeah,' said Fulton, finished his beer and straightened up. 'I'm goin' to think over what you just said. You might be right because it's a lead-pipe cinch those two aren't taking any back seat in this even though they're tryin' to make me think they are.'

Fulton left the saloon, went to the jailhouse and found that the hotel-clerk had dumped a stack of mail upon his desk there. He sat down and rifled through what turned out to be mostly wanted posters. There were two letters. One was from a woman in Idaho seeking a lost husband. The other was from a man down in Texas seeking a lost daughter. To the first letter Fulton gave his attention only briefly; the description of the missing man was so general it would have fit two-thirds of the cowboys and townsmen in Oklahoma Territory. He put that letter aside.

The second letter was more explicit. It

described the man's daughter so well that Fulton stopped reading half way through and flipped the page to see the signature: Alfred Short!

Fulton gently leaned back, tipped up his hat, glanced out into the dusky roadway where lights were coming on here and there, and let off a long, quiet sigh. There was no need to read the rest of the letter but he read it anyway. It told him that Barbara's father thought she might have run off with a young cowboy named Anthony Quayle, a lad, so the letter said, who was related to the powerful Bosworth and Quayle cattle-interest families of the southern Pecos country.

Fulton folded this letter and placed it carefully into a shirt pocket. He sat for almost a half hour with his feet cocked up, his hat tipped back, and his solemn gaze lying out across the roadway towards the hotel's front entrance which was framed in the jailhouse doorway. Eventually he saw young Quayle come sauntering along. He had two packages in his hands and although Fulton couldn't make out his expression in the dusk, he thought he knew what that expression would be—a little quiet half-smile.

He didn't move for some time after Tony had entered the hotel, but eventually he arose, stepped out into the cool evening, and instead of hiking on over to the hotel, he turned southward and paced down through Ione's lower environs to a small, neat cottage painted white, passed through the picket gate and went up on to the front porch. There, out of the quiet shadows, a man's pleasant voice spoke over to him from a cluster of chairs.

'Good evening, Marshal. Come sit down. I don't often get to see you.'

Fulton caught that innuendo and went across to where the older man sat, smiling up at him. This was the Reverend Charles Steen, a man in his early fifties who had snow-white hair and the rosy, unlined cheeks of blooming youth. Fulton sat down. There was a flourishing honeysuckle vine growing up one corner of the porch and its fragrance was almost overpowering.

'Beautiful night, Marshal. Look at that sky. Clear as glass.'

Fulton looked up and looked down again. He said, 'Reverend; you performed any marriages lately?'

Steen turned to serenely regard Fulton. 'Performed one today, Marshal, as a matter of fact. Fine young couple. The boy was quite handsome and the girl was—'

'Small and taffy-haired and violet-eyed,' murmured Fulton dourly, looking out into the settling night.

'That's right, Marshal. Why; is there something wrong?'

Instead of replying Fulton drew forth that letter from his pocket and passed it over. The

Reverend Steen put on a pair of steel-rimmed spectacles, held the letter up to catch what meagre light was available, and carefully read, then re-read, the letter. He afterwards methodically folded his spectacles, put them in his pocket and handed back the letter without speaking.

'Well, Reverend . . . ?'

Steen pursed his lips, faintly frowned, and said, 'Well, Marshal—it's in the hands of the Lord.'

Fulton shook his head. 'Uh huh,' he dissented. 'It's in the hands of a lot less infallible person—me.'

'She gave her age as twenty, Marshal. That's past the age of legal consent.'

'Tell her folks that, Reverend.' Fulton stood up, tossed the letter into Steen's lap and stepped over to porch's edge. Then he turned and put a thoughtful look upon the minister. 'The address is there, Reverend. You write 'em and tell them that today you married their daughter to young Anthony Quayle.'

'But Marshal, my job is only to—'

'I know, Reverend; your job is only to unite in holy matrimony whom God hath brought together. Well; I'd say that the bringin' together in holy matrimony doesn't end when you collect your fee and close the Book. I'd say it includes trying to make peace between the girl, the boy, and her folks down in Texas. Good night, Reverend.'

Fulton went back out to the boardwalk, turned without a rearward glance, and walked along loosely, tiredly, as far as the hotel. As he entered the night-clerk perked up, saying, 'You find that mail I tossed on your desk?'

Fulton nodded. 'I found it. Thanks. Thanks a lot.' He saw a big, older man sitting in the lobby's solitary overstuffed chair reading a newspaper. This man's stiff-brimmed black Texas hat was lying carelessly atop a little table near the man's elbow. Beyond that one man the lobby was empty. Fulton headed for the stairway and started up it. At the landing he stepped clear and started to cross over towards his door when a quiet voice came at him out of the shadows.

'Evenin', Marshal. Saw you walkin' along outside and thought I'd wait for you.'

Fulton turned. Tony Quayle was leaning upon the wall ten feet away, his clear, slate-coloured eyes faintly smiling.

Fulton balanced the door key in his hand steadily gazing at Quayle saying nothing. His feelings toward this younger man were mixed.

'Thought I'd tell you it's all right from now on if I'm in Barbara's room or if she's in my room.'

Fulton said quietly, 'Yes, I know. I just had a little discussion with Reverend Steen. Tell me something, Tony; why did you wait for three days after you arrived in Ione to do it?'

'Had to, Marshal. You see, it took that long

for my best man to arrive here.' Young Quayle smiled. 'But that's not the only reason I been waiting for you, Marshal. I thought over some of the stuff you told me yesterday an' last night. You're right. I had no business gettin' mad. You were plumb right an' I appreciate what you've been trying to do.'

Fulton considered; his feelings towards this young Texan were still mixed. Tony Quayle was one of those men it was just as easy to dislike as it was to like; he made no overtures, offered no friendship, showed nothing outwardly except that little faint half-wise, half-arrogant smile. Fulton flipped his door key, caught it and turned it over in his fingers examining it. Finally he said, 'Your wife's folks wrote a letter to the law here in Ione, Tony. They said they thought she'd run off with you. I gathered from that letter they weren't too fond of the idea of her marrying you.'

'I know, Marshal; that's my fault too. When they gave me arguments I laughed at them, gave her the money to run away on, and met her two towns north of Pecos, then we came here. They got reason to feel bitter towards me, Marshal; I didn't handle the thing right. That's what we were talkin' about last night when you came along.' Quayle straightened up off the wall, his eyes for once sober and relenting. 'I'll straighten that out an' if I have to eat crow, I'll eat it. Only I loved her.' Tony looked straight over at Fulton. 'Does this make much sense to you?'

'It makes sense, Tony. It makes a lot of sense. I guess you'll do to ride the rimrocks with. But I sure had my doubts for a few days.'

'Yeah. It's that first impression. Barbara's told me about that. She says I antagonise folks by acting the way I do. Well, hell; if I have to change I'll do it, that's all.' Tony stepped over and pushed out his right hand. 'How about a fresh deal between us, Marshal?'

Fulton put his key in his left hand, shook, and slowly smiled. 'Done,' he said. 'Does this give me the right to kiss the bride?'

Tony's face broke into that boyish grin. 'It sure does. Tomorrow some of our friends'll be here for a little supper. I'd look right kindly on it if you'd be there too.'

Fulton nodded. 'Be happy to,' he said, and turned to insert the key into his door. 'Didn't know you'd made any friends here in town, Tony.'

'Not local friends, Marshal. These are from my paw's trail-herd. They're the folks we waited here in Ione to meet.'

Fulton felt like he'd just been kicked in the stomach by an army mule. He slowly turned, his smile gone, and looked steadily at young Quayle. 'Your paw's trail-herd?' he softly asked.

'Yeah. You see, Barbi and I timed it so's we'd meet the drive here at Ione, get married with my paw for best man an' with my sister

71

along to sort of chaperon us on our way north with the drive after we were married.'

'Your paw owns that Texas herd north of town, Tony?'

'Yes. He rode in this morning, stood up for me down at that preacher's house, then he got a room here at the hotel for the night, an' tomorrow we'll all three of us ride back out, catch up with the herd and head on out for the Kansas plains. In fact, my paw was up here just a few minutes ago.'

Fulton said, 'Big man, Tony, wearin' a tweed coat and a stiff-brimmed, black Texas hat?'

'That's him. You met him already, Marshal?'

Fulton shook his head. 'I'll meet him in the morning. You three figure to have breakfast together before you head for the herd?'

'Yeah.'

'Fine,' said Fulton softly. 'I'll see you then. Good night, Tony.'

'Good night, Marshal.'

Fulton entered his room, didn't light the lamp, crossed over and stood for a long while gazing down into the night-shadowed roadway. Maybe a man who'd just married off his son wouldn't object to buying his passage across MF range, and then again he might object. What a hell of a way for newlyweds to start married life—smack in the middle of a fight!

CHAPTER EIGHT

Fulton took his time about dressing in the morning. When he eventually appeared in the dining-room doorway of the hotel he saw Tony and Barbara and the large, heavy man he'd seen the night before reading that paper in the lobby. They also saw him; he saw Tony's lips move and the older man's leonine head swing half around. Fulton and Tony's father studied one another as the marshal strode on over.

The elder Quayle was a rock-like man with the ruddy face and testy flash to his eyes that seemed always to go with these wealthy Texas cattlemen. He stood up and shook with Fulton, caught a chair from an adjoining table and swung it forward. His first name was Travis, a common name among Texans whose shrine where their particular heroes including William Barrett Travis had perished in the bloody war for Texas independence, had made its deep imprint on every succeeding generation, and was their hallowed Alamo.

Fulton gazed a moment upon Barbara. Her eyes were misty with a softness that cut him under the heart. He smiled at her and when the waiter came Fulton ordered his usual breakfast; a quart of black coffee, fried meat and fried potatoes.

Travis Quayle ordered the same and threw

an expansive smile at Fulton. 'Always liked a man who ate like one,' he rumbled, and Fulton's heart sank at the blunt roughness of that voice. This man, in a different way, was another Big Jim Morton. He was ruthless and hard as iron; he was also wealthy and powerful. But here the difference came in; Travis Quayle, in Fulton's careful assessment, was not a man to mince words, condone dishonesty—or pay passage over free-graze land!

Fulton settled himself upon the chair, put aside his hat, looked straight at Tony's father and said, 'I think you're going to have to change your plans this morning, Mister Quayle. Marsh'll be along directly to explain why.'

All three people at the table with Fulton looked up at him. Travis Quayle's expression showed bewilderment. He said, 'How's that, Marshal; change my plans—how?'

Fulton dragged back a big breath and explained about the blockading cattlemen, about his meeting with them in the company of Travis Quayle's trail-boss. Then he told the big Texan about Big Jim Morton's passage fee, and as he spoke on, he saw Travis Quayle's jaw lock down hard, saw those testy eyes begin to flame, saw that long-lipped mouth, so much like Tony's mouth in shape, turn fierce and uncompromising.

'I'll not pay,' Travis Quayle said, finally, his

74

voice choked with wrath. 'I'll not give this MF outfit a single damned red cent, Marshal!'

Their breakfasts came and for as long as it took the waiter to set things down they sat silent, but the moment he departed Travis Quayle said, 'A nickel a head is the rule, and usually that's for damage to planted crops, Marshal. Two bits a head is highway robbery.'

Fulton picked up his coffee cup. 'Marsh said the same thing yesterday, Mister Travis.' Fulton avoided the two younger faces as he sipped and set the cup back down. He had ruined their first breakfast as married people; it made him feel like something dirty. 'Morton, Fisk, and I reckon the others'll be along in a little while to meet with you over at my office, Mister Travis. That's why I said you'd have to change your plans this morning.' Fulton looked soberly down at his laden plate; he wasn't hungry at all, now.

'There's something else I've got to tell you, Mister Travis,' he said. 'Don't make trouble. Pay up or not as you see fit, but don't start any trouble. My part in this is about like a critter caught between two trees; I can't do any more than try to keep both of 'em apart. I wish I could, but I can't.' He stood up, dredged up a silver dollar, dropped it beside his untouched plate of food and looked straight down into Barbara's uplifted face. 'I'm sorry. I'd have almost been willin' to chop off an arm before doing this on your first breakfast as a married

75

lady. But I had no other choice.'

He turned and walked back out of the diningroom with his hat in his left hand, with his ivory-butted .45 swaying outwards as he strode on through the lobby and emerged upon the yonder sidewalk. There, he put his hat on, and there too, he met Ab Slaughter on his way to open up the saloon. Ab halted, squinted at Fulton's freshly-brushed black coat, pants and hat, then he raised his eyes to Fulton's troubled face and checked himself in whatever he had been going to say, and said instead, 'You're out kind of early this morning, Bob; anything wrong?'

'Nothing's right,' said Fulton, and stepped down into the dust to begin pacing on across towards the jailhouse.

He didn't quite make it; a jogging horseman came along and called ahead. Fulton turned, stepped up in front of his office and recognised Hudson Marsh. With Marsh were two men Fulton recognised instantly: Fred Whorton and Joel Dunlap. The three of them came abreast, reined up and gazed at Fulton for a moment before Marsh said, 'Them others showed up yet?'

'No,' Fulton replied, 'but your boss is over at the hotel having breakfast with his son and his new daughter-in-law.'

'Oh; you met 'em already, eh?'

Fulton said stonily, 'I met 'em. I also told them about Jim Morton's passage fee.'

'And?' inquired Marsh, showing quick interest.

'And—I don't think he's going to pay it, Marsh. You better go over and talk to him.'

'He's *got* to pay it!'

Fulton said grimly, 'Don't tell me, tell *him*,' turned on his heel and entered the jailhouse.

Reverend Charles Steen came into Fulton's office with a letter in his hand. He teetered in the doorway as though uncertain both of his welcome and of his mission. Fulton, shuffling through wanted posters, looked up as that thin shadow obstructed his light expecting to see Fisk or Morton, gazed mildly at the minister and leaned back.

'Come in, Reverend; what's on your mind?'

'I've answered the letter of that young lady's parents down in Texas and wondered if you'd like to read it before I send it off.'

Fulton emphatically shook his head. 'That's your affair,' he said. 'I washed my hands of it when I gave you their letter.' As he finished speaking he heard horsemen coming on down the road, stood up, stepped past Steen and looked out. Big Jim Morton, Buckley Fisk, Carleton Whitney and four other cattlemen were passing slowly down towards the jailhouse. Over across the road upon the opposite plankwalk, also watching those riders, stood Travis Quayle, his son, Hudson Marsh and the two Texas cowboys. None of these latter men made any attempt to walk on over

77

until after Morton and his companions had tied up at Fulton's jailhouse hitchrack and tramped on inside. Then they moved out.

Fulton made way for Morton, Fisk, Whitney and their friends to enter his office. Afterwards, seeing Quayle's crew approaching he turned and shot Reverend Steen an impatient look, saying, 'Go post your letter.'

Travis Quayle went past Fulton without glancing at him. So did Marsh, Whorton and Dunlap. But Tony Quayle looked straight into Fulton's dark eyes, and gently nodded. Steen walked away and Fulton closed his office door, stood with his shoulders against it watching those wooden, tough faces, then made the bare minimum in introductions. No one offered to shake hands but Big Jim slowly nodded each time one of Quayle's men was named. Then Big Jim said in a quieter tone than was his custom, 'Mister Quayle, I reckon you know the terms for passin' over MF range.'

Travis Quayle, as large a man physically as Big Jim, met the other's impassive look with a cold start. 'I know the terms,' he replied flintily, 'and I'll pay you the going rate, which is five cents a head.'

Buckley Fisk stirred, hooked both thumbs in his shell-belt and coldly studied Travis Quayle. Fulton had the impression, watching Buckley, that Big Jim and his pardner had reached an agreement before coming to this meeting, and

78

that Buckley was not to enter into the negotiations at all; at least not for as long as things were in the talking stage. But Fulton knew Buckley Fisk; if there was trouble Buckley would be in the thick of it. He meant to keep a close watch on Fisk.

'Well now,' said Big Jim to Travis Quayle. 'That's plumb out of the question. Like we told your range-boss yesterday, that grass is worth three times that to us, just for grazing.'

Travis Quayle looked around into those other faces. He considered quiet, gaunt Buckley Fisk the longest, evidently making a judgement here, then he swung back towards Fulton and said, 'What's the law say in matters like this, Marshal? In Texas I could tell you, but this isn't Texas.'

'It sure isn't,' one of those cattlemen over behind Big Jim murmured, and this brought Quayle's big leonine head whipping back around. Whoever said that was utterly quiet in the face of Quayle's challenging glare.

Fulton moved away from the door, crossed to his desk and leaned there. 'I'm here to keep the peace,' said Fulton, gazing around at those opposing factions. 'That's all. I can't say who is right and who isn't; that's not my job. Maybe you men need a couple of lawyers and a judge.'

'Time,' said Hudson Marsh. 'Time is something we're running out of, Marshal. We got no time to get lawyers and such-like.'

'Then pay the two-bits,' said Big Jim. 'It's

not goin' to break anyone. But it'll help Buckley an' me recover from the loss of our grass.'

Quayle turned to Marsh. 'How much of their range are the animals spread out over?' he demanded.

Marsh shrugged. 'I couldn't rightly say; maybe a section. Maybe two sections. We've been holdin' 'em bunched up as best we can.'

Quayle turned back toward Big Jim. 'What's land worth in this part of Oklahoma?'

Morton hung fire over his answer. Carleton Whitney shifted his stance and frowned at the floor. Several of the other cattlemen with Morton and Fisk also looked uncomfortable.

Fulton could answer this; he'd made appraisals for the adjudicating committees on land titles. He said, 'Twenty-five cents an acre for grass-land.'

Big Jim spoke up quickly now, saying, 'Hell, Marshal; that can't be right.'

Fulton shrugged. 'The government thinks it is, Jim. Furthermore, if you want to make a land issue out of this instead of an issue of right-of-way, let's talk about titles to that land.'

Buckley Fisk's deaths-head face whipped around. 'You shut up,' he snapped at Fulton. 'You got a badge an' that's all you got. A minute ago you said all you was here for was to keep the peace. Then don't start buttin' in where your black nose don't belong.'

Fulton saw how the discussion's adverse

80

turning had angered Buckley. He also saw that Buckley was losing patience with all this talk. And although he felt no rush of anger at Buckley's words, which surprised him a little since Fisk had obviously made it a point to belittle him in front of all these men, he said, 'Take off your gun Buckley. You're cocked and primed, so just take off that gun and I'll oblige you.'

Big Jim jumped in here, saying in that oily way he sometimes spoke, 'No call for that, boys, no call at all. I'm a peaceable man. The last thing I want is trouble. The last thing any of us cowmen want is trouble. Before we'd have that we'd let the cattle through without them payin' a thin dime.'

Fulton, Quayle, even Carleton Whitney and the others, all looked dumbfoundedly at Big Jim. This was such an abrupt about-face, all thought of that former antagonism was lost sight of for the interval of astonished silence which ensued.

Travis Quayle finally said, obviously believing Jim Morton was sincere, 'Well hell, Morton; I'm not an unreasonable man. I'll split it down the middle with you. I'll pay twelve an' a half cents a head to cross on out of the Ione country.'

Fulton stood there staring at Big Jim. When his amazement had passed he began having some second thoughts. For four years he'd watched Morton and Fisk operate. For four years he'd heard all manner of talk about those two, and none of it had ever been at all like this thing he'd just witnessed. Big Jim was not being benevolent, Fulton was convinced of that. Then what was he up to?

'Done,' said Morton in that booming way of his, to Travis Quayle. 'And all us southwestern Oklahoma cattlemen ask is that in the future you find some other way around our land, Mister Quayle.'

Hudson Marsh said dryly, 'At twelve cents a head we couldn't afford to use this route too often, Mister Morton.'

That remark, spoken the way it was, very dry and very soft, broke the tension. Carleton Whitney made a relieved little chuckle, which acted almost as a signal for everyone else to laugh a little and smile back and forth.

All but lanky Buckley Fisk. He looked as disapproving as ever over there with his thumbs hooked low in his gun-belt, and as the others began filing back out of Fulton's office, Buckley was the last to go.

Fulton nailed him in the doorway. 'Buck,' he said, 'I want a word with you.'

The others walked on, were beyond hearing. They were moving in a loose body in the direction of Ab Slaughter's saloon.

'Take off the gun, Buck.'

Now Fisk did something which was entirely out of character for him too. He smiled at Fulton, and said, 'I apologise, Marshal. I take it all back.' Then, still smiling, he turned and also walked away.

Fulton went to the door staring after Fisk, astonished but suddenly very uneasy. He began to wonder if everything those two had said and done hadn't been rehearsed beforehand. It seemed suspiciously as though this were the case. He had never before even heard of Buckley Fisk back down from a fight, nor Big Jim Morton reversing any stand he'd taken.

Gradually Fulton turned and moved back to his desk. He sat down there, was still sitting there looking plainly disturbed, when young Tony Quayle appeared suddenly in the doorway.

'Hey Marshal; aren't you comin' along? We're all going to have a drink over at the saloon.'

Fulton's gaze cleared a little. He said, 'No thanks. But I'll see you around town later.'

Tony's hint of an habitual smile came up. 'Sure,' he retorted. 'Over at the hotel diningroom at high noon. The others'll be there too.' Tony made a little casual salute with his right hand and stepped away, turned and went hurrying back up the plankwalk.

Fulton got up, rummaged his desk for a smoke, found a cigar and lighted it. The longer he thought on it the stronger became his conviction that there was something seriously wrong here. But try as he might he couldn't put his finger upon it.

Men like Morton and Fisk just did not in sincerity act like this. They were up to something, there was no doubt about that, but what was it? He went over, leaned in the open doorway and quietly smoked, quietly watched mid-day come to Ione in off the open range far out.

CHAPTER NINE

Big Jim took Buckley Fisk and his other companions out of Ione a little after mid-day riding west. They had a long way to go and although the days were longer now it would still be long after dark before most of them reached home.

Marshal Fulton was at his desk a little later when Travis Quayle strode in, looked down his big nose and made a rueful smile at the marshal as he stepped up, took a chair and dropped down upon it.

'I paid 'em,' Quayle said gruffly, obviously speaking of the Ione cattlemen. 'I didn't like it even a little bit but I paid 'em.' Quayle fished out a fresh cigar, offered it to Fulton, and when he got back a negative headshake the big Texan bit off the cigar's wrapped end, rammed it between his heavy teeth and lit up. 'What they really wanted was for one of us to have quit coming up this way.' Quayle exhaled and smacked his lips over the good bite of that strong tobacco. 'All right; we'll find another way. There's still a lot of open country from here to the Kansas plains.'

Fulton leaned back watching this gruff, raw Texan and wondering if Quayle, who had to be a good judge of men being in the business he was in, had found anything that rang false about Big Jim Morton. Then Quayle said something that made Fulton understand how Quayle had been able to overlook Morton's palpable falseness. He said, 'You know, Marshal, when a man's only got one boy, and that boy gets married, it sort of tugs at the heartstrings a little. I've been a widower fifteen years; since Tony was a boy an' his sister wasn't much older. It's been a long row to hoe since then, and today—well—today was some kind of a milestone. It took me back a long ways, Marshal.'

Fulton allowed Quayle to ramble on. Clearly, the big Texan was in a mellow mood. But after a while Fulton spoke up, saying, 'Miss Barbara's paw wrote me a letter, Mister Quayle. He didn't like the idea of this marriage.'

Quayle made an easy gesture with his cigar. 'I know. I knew all about that before I left Texas. But the boy's all right, Marshal. He won't ever do anything to hurt little Barbi. As for Al Short—when we get back I'll go see him

85

myself. He's a good man; just got off somehow on the wrong foot with Tony.'

Fulton had said his say on this score and put it out of his mind. He was turning back to the matter of Morton when someone appeared silently in the open doorway drawing Fulton's sweeping dark gaze swiftly upwards.

A girl was standing there; a tall, square-shouldered girl with pale gold hair and slate-grey eyes the colour of oak smoke against a wintery sky. She had a long mouth that had an upward tilt at its outer corners and a centre heaviness. Framed in that rough doorway she looked to Fulton to be both delicate and somehow strong as iron. He didn't miss the similarity in her features and the features of Travis Quayle, but he sat there without moving, held still and awed by her beauty and her smoky, dead-level gaze.

For a moment longer Travis Quayle did not know she was behind him, and for the full run of that moment she gazed straight at Bob Fulton, and he at her. There was something bold in her expression, as though she recognised Fulton for a full man and dared him to break the assurance, the calm poise, of her gaze. As though she saw in him nothing more, at first anyway, than simply another raw man from a raw environment.

Then that expression broke, turned interested, turned appraising and curious. That was when Quayle, looking at Fulton, followed the marshal's gaze around and saw the girl behind him, and jumped up.

'Hello, honey,' he rumbled at her. 'Come in, come in. Marshal; this is my daughter Belle. Honey, this is U.S. Marshal Fulton.'

She barely nodded, her wintry gaze holding steadily to Fulton's face. He removed his hat and made a little gallant bow from the waist. In its dark place his heart was solidly drumming; she was beautiful; the longer he looked the more flawless, clean and wholesome that beauty seemed. There was a little sprinkling of freckles across the saddle of her nose and the firm flesh of her throat visible above her snow-white blouse, was golden tan from days in the sun.

Suddenly Fulton knew where he'd seen this beautiful girl before; driving the 'possible' wagon in the drag of that Texas trail-herd the day before. He said something about this too, and saw those wintry eyes brighten a little in an ironic smile.

'I remember too, Marshal,' she said. 'You rode straight up the sidehill and stopped twice to rest your animal. I remember because you were wearing a black Prince Albert coat and an ivory-handled gun; it made a very striking, very romantic picture. When I was a little girl down home I used to imagine that's what young Lochinvar probably would have looked like.'

Fulton thought there was some underlying

87

meaning here; thought she was slyly chiding him. He said, 'Well Miss Belle; what I remember about you is that you were wearing a white shirt while riding in the drag of a herd, and didn't have a neckerchief up over your face.'

Travis Quayle, looking from one to the other, began to very slowly lose his look of genial condescension. As he watched his daughter's creamy face remain fully forward, her slate-grey gaze unwaveringly upon the Oklahoma lawman, Quayle seemed to become troubled. He finally broke in, saying, 'Well; were you looking for me, honey?' And his daughter murmured, 'Tony is over at the hotel, paw,' and kept right on considering Bob Fulton.

Quayle looked back and forth, his uneasiness becoming increasingly evident. 'Then we'd better be going along,' he said to Belle.

'The marshal's supposed to come too, paw. Those were Tony's last orders to me—bring along the marshal.'

Quayle said a trifle testily, 'Well hell; let's get going then,' and made no move to head for the door until Fulton broke it off, looked over at the older man, instantly read the signs there of a gathering storm, and dropped his hat back on as he crossed over towards the doorway where Travis Quayle's daughter lightly stepped outside making room for him.

Those two waited a moment until Belle's father was also upon the outside plankwalk, then they turned and strolled on out into the mid-day heat side by side. Quayle, lumbering along behind, furiously puffed his cigar and glowered; they were acting as though they'd known each other all their lives and it seemed somehow indecent to him. But he said nothing; he glared and stamped on over to the hotel entrance, but he said nothing at all.

Hudson Marsh was in the diningroom doorway freshly shaved, scrubbed, and attired in clean clothing. Joel Dunlap and Fred Whorton were also there. They seemed to be particularly close friends of young Tony Quayle. The only other girl in that large room excepting Belle Quayle was little Barbara; her face was flushed, her eyes were shiny-bright, and as each man stepped up to peck her on the cheek and gallantly say something, Barbara's colour came and went.

Fulton stopped in the doorway feeling that little pain under his heart again. Then he moved on. Belle left him to cross over and say something to her brother. Travis Quayle moved up and carefully considered his cigar before he said, 'Marshal; sometimes a man feels a loss more than he lets on.' Fulton looked around, not understanding this remark at all, but Travis Quayle walked away leaving that little enigmatic comment hanging there.

Barbara came over and smiled up at Fulton.

He removed his hat, bent stiffly and kissed her cheek, then he said, his words with just a hint of a little drag to them, sounding very soft, 'I wish you the best of everything, Miss Barbara, and anyway that I can ever help . . .' he paused, felt colour mounting up under his cheeks, and smiled lamely. She touched his arm lightly.

'You've already helped, Marshal. And we were strangers.'

Tony came over. He had a quizzical look to his glance. 'I heard you almost had a fight after the meeting this morning, Marshal. After we'd all walked out except that skinny Fisk feller.'

Fulton was startled. 'Where did you hear that?' he demanded.

'Fisk told about it over at the saloon. Said you asked him to take off his gun again. Said he apologised to you.'

Fulton got a faint vertical line between his dark brows but he brushed this topic aside because it wasn't fitting. He only said, 'I wish I could figure those two out, Tony.'

'Forget it, Marshal. We paid. That's the end of it.' Tony took Barbara's hand in his and held it. He smiled. 'You met my sister. She just told me. She's over at the punch bowl. Why don't you go on over?'

Fulton said, 'Thanks; reckon I will,' and stepped away. Tony watched him cross through the noisy room, dropped his head and whispered something to Barbara that made her eyes spring wide open. She breathed, 'No;

I don't believe it, Tony.'

Travis Quayle had hired the entire hotel diningroom, staff and all. It was a much larger room for this little reception than was needed, but if noise could fill up the vacant places, then it was none too large. Hudson Marsh was beaming. It struck Fulton that this rock-hard, burly trail-boss had his soft side exactly as his boss also had.

Dunlap and Whorton were with Belle when Fulton came along. They smiled at him with what he thought was just the slightest bit of reserve, and drifted away from the punch-bowl table. Just for a second Belle's smoky eyes darkened over this, then she held up a glass cup for Fulton. He took it, thanked her, and put his back to the bowl as he looked around. She said, 'Marshal; what's troubling you?'

Surprised, he looked around and down. 'Is something troubling me, ma'm?' he mildly asked.

She nodded, her dead-level gaze intent upon his face. 'You're thinking I don't know you well enough to say that. But Marshal, I was raised by men. My mother died when I was quite young. I've known your kind before.'

'What kind is that, ma'm?' asked Fulton, turning interested.

'The kind that keeps most things locked up inside them. The thoughtful, observant, wise kind, Marshal.'

Fulton felt his colour rising again. He

chuckled to offset this, but he felt uneasy. 'No particular trouble, Miss Belle. Just something that doesn't sit well with me.'

'Morton and Fisk?'

He was surprised for the second time. 'You met them?'

She shook her head. 'They were riding out of town as I was riding in. But I saw them.'

'I see. And you know *their* kind too.'

Belle's smile lost a little of its warmth. 'Very well, Marshal. So does my father. So does Hudson Marsh.'

Fulton put aside his untouched cup of punch. He said, 'Are you telling me something, Miss Belle?'

She shook her head up at him. 'No, not particularly. Not now. This is Tony's and Barbi's big day. We can't spoil it, can we?'

He stood there gravely considering this beautiful girl. There was something disquieting about her; something that seemed almost masculine, the way she thought, the way she spoke. He'd never before come across a woman he could speak to as he'd speak to a man, and it left him a little unsettled.

She hooked her hand inside his arm and moved out. 'Come along, Marshal. Tomorrow is another day. This one belongs to Tony and Barbi. Let's help them remember it as something very special for as long as they live.'

Now, Fulton thought, she was being a typical woman. He allowed her to lead him

92

over where the others were. Once, he caught her father's steady gaze upon them. Another time he saw Barbara gazing at him strangely too. Then it was time to eat.

Tony made a little speech which surprised Fulton because, for all his worldliness, Tony was awkward and clumsy at this. But it made Fulton like him better.

Barbara was called upon also, but she couldn't even do as well as her husband had done so Travis Quayle stood up, waited for absolute silence, then offered a solemn toast. Everyone drank, and across from Belle Quayle, Fulton caught her grey gaze over the rims of their glasses, and slowly smiled. She intrigued him; not just her uncommon beauty, but the way she had of saying things, of looking straight to the core of things as a man did.

She smiled back.

CHAPTER TEN

It was a special occasion and might have run on all that afternoon, Fulton was never to know how it otherwise might have ended because Ab Slaughter suddenly loomed up out in the doorway making faces and imperious gestures. Fulton excused himself and went over to Ab.

'What's wrong with you?' he demanded. 'Can't you see this is a private party, Ab?'

'I can see what it is all right,' snapped the saloonman. 'But I got somethin' to tell you. One of those Texas hands from that herd north of town just come in more dead than alive an' I got him up at my place. You better come listen to what he's got to say.'

Fulton's stomach muscles squeezed up. He and Ab exchanged a charged look then Ab frowningly turned away and Fulton went along in Ab's wake.

As they left the hotel, turned right and headed for the saloon Fulton caught up. 'What is it?' he asked.

Ab snapped one word: 'Trouble.' Then he thought this over and said, 'Trouble in spades, Bob. That herd was hit and stampeded from hell to breakfast.'

Fulton looked at his companion without uttering a word. They were within fifty feet of the saloon before Ab slowed, looked around and shook his head. 'This one's goin' to die,' he said, dropping his voice. 'I don't see how he ever got this far. He's shot through the lights from left to right.'

They entered the bar. There was a sprinkling of men in there; it was too early in the day for any serious drinking, but the men who *were* there weren't drinking, they were standing around speaking a little, looking grim and acting stiff.

Ab took the marshal past the bar and through a small doorway into a back room. Here, where his swamper had a cot, were two men standing beside another man. Fulton didn't recognise this cowboy but could easily tell by looking that the injured cowboy was a Texan. The others moved back as Fulton strode up. One of them had his sleeves rolled. He had a basin of pink water in one hand. The other man, without speaking a word, bent, pointed to a puffy little puncture in the Texan's left side high up, traced the course of this hole across the wounded man's chest and showed Fulton where the bullet had exited. Then he stepped back again.

Fulton looked into the cowboy's face. It was very grey, very slack. The man did not appear to be in any great pain; he seemed simply to be sinking fast and in the grip of a powerful lethargy. He was young and boyish with coppery red hair and a day's growth of the same colour beard. His eyes were a muddy shade of green. They looked straight up as Marshal Fulton bent down. They made a little shadowy smile but showed no recognition at all.

Fulton said his name and who he was. He then asked what had happened. The cowboy's head rolled faintly. He ran out his tongue, brushed numb lips with it, and said, 'Hit us like Injuns. Hit us from the east with the sun at their backs an' in our eyes. Come out of that damned canyon yellin' and shootin'.'

'Who were they?' Fulton asked quickly, seeing the man slowly wilt under his eyes. 'Did you know any of them?'

'No. Strangers. Maybe—dozen of 'em. Had all the advantage. Stampeded them cattle like a flock of crows. Scattered for ten miles by now. Where's Hud? Hey Hud, you here? Listen; somethin' I want you to do for me, Hud . . .'

The voice turned thick, and faded down to a soft, long sigh. The Texan was dead.

One of those men standing back murmured a soft, 'Amen,' and turned to tiptoe out of the room. His companion also departed. Fulton straightened up, looked across at Ab, and said, 'Well; there are probably other ones out there also hurt. I'd better go saddle up.'

'You'd better make up a posse,' said Ab tartly.

Fulton gazed downward. 'Young,' he said quietly. 'Pretty young for going out like that, Ab.'

'That's not what's giving me the willies, Bob. What's that big Texan going to say when he hears about this—and sees his cowboy lyin' here dead?'

Fulton raised his eyes. 'Do me a favour, Ab. Go get Quayle and fetch him up here.'

Ab said, 'Sure,' and left the room.

Fulton bent over, rummaged the dead Texan's pockets, found a little money and a gold watch with an inscription inside its front cover which read 'To William From Mother and Father'. There was also the date. Fulton stood holding that watch; it was still warm to the touch and quietly ticking. One line from the *Cowboy's Lament* came to haunt him.

. . . He'll not see his mother when the works all done this fall . . .

He turned as the heavy footfalls of a large man approaching sounded loud in the hush, and when Travis Quayle loomed up filling the doorway Fulton saw in the older man's face that Ab had told him.

He let Travis stand there staring at the dead man for several long moments, then he held out the watch. 'Be better if you keep this. These things have a way of disappearing between now and burial-time.' He also handed Travis Quayle the little wad of crushed bills.

For a long time Quayle just stood there holding the watch and money before he stepped farther into the room. Until he did that Fulton didn't catch sight of Ab behind him.

'Who did it, Marshal?' Quayle asked, his gaze lifting so that Fulton could see its odd milkiness.

'He didn't say; only that they came out of the canyon with the sun behind them shooting and yelling. It's pretty clear what they had in mind—stampeding your herd.'

'But why?' Quayle asked. Then he said

97

something which showed he'd already made up his mind who'd done this. 'I paid 'em. I made peace and paid 'em.'

'It doesn't necessarily have to have been the local cattlemen, Mister Quayle.'

'Then who? And Will here; hell, this was only his second trip up the trail. Why would anyone want to kill him?'

Fulton didn't answer because he knew Quayle's shock was making him ask questions which he'd know the answers to as soon as he recovered from his surprise.

Fulton said, 'I want you to send me Hudson Marsh. None of the others, just Marsh. And I want you not to say anything about this to Tony or the others for at least an hour.'

Quayle looked puzzled. He saw a chair, went over and dropped down upon it. 'Where's the herd?' he asked dumbly, staring at the dead rangerider.

'It's scattered. Listen to me, Mister Quayle. I'm going up there. I want to do some tracking if I can. But if you and the others also go charging out there it'll play hob with any tracks I may find, so don't say anything for an hour. Give me that much of a start.'

Quayle raised his hand and looked at the watch, then very suddenly he stood up, his expression completely altered, and he was over his shock. He looked straight at Fulton and said, his tone roughening, turning fierce and vengeful, 'I figure we'd *all* better ride up there,

98

Marshal.'

Fulton recognised the futility of arguing and said nothing. Quayle started for the door, paused once as though he expected Fulton to try and stop him, looked at the lawman, at Ab Slaughter, then went swiftly on out of the room. The moment he was out of sight Fulton said to Ab, 'Come on; we can beat their time if we hurry and I want to be up there ahead of him.'

'Me?' said Ab, astonished.

'Yeah you. Come on.'

Ab looked uneasy about this, but when Fulton hiked on out he trailed after him.

Out in the saloon a large number of men were standing around. Evidently the word had spread already that one of the Quayle trailhands had been badly shot up and was lying at Slaughter's saloon, for while the bartender was handy, not very many of those townsmen were drinking.

Fulton and Ab pushed through hurriedly, struck the yonder plankwalk and made straight on over to the liverybarn. There, with hurried explanations each man rigged out a horse and with the liveryman standing back looking astonished, they stepped up, booted their beasts out, and headed north on out of town.

For two miles after they'd left Ione neither the marshal nor the saloonman attempted to talk back and forth, but when it became necessary to slow their mounts Ab said, 'I only got my little derringer, Bob. If there's any shootin' I'll be about as useful as horns on a man.'

Fulton shrugged. The matter of individual armament didn't seem important to him right then. He was thinking back, trying to recall the hour that Big Jim and the cattlemen had left town, then work forward from there and see if it was possible for them to have gotten to Ambush Canyon from the eastern entrance, gone down the canyon and struck the Texas herd.

He concluded that they probably could have done it but they'd have had to have ridden hard. But something else bothered him about this; Morton and Fisk were not in his opinion the least bit above committing such an act, but he'd known Carleton Whitney a long time. Whitney was just not the ambushing type. One or two of the other ranchers with Whitney weren't either, and yet all those men had left town together.

Then he began sifting through the riders employed by those men, and here it was not at all difficult to come up with some faces and names belonging to men who not only would have hit the Quayle herd like this, but probably had in fact actually done so. On every range there was an element of tough men who would break the law, even kill, for no better reason than to be in on the excitement. The problem was going to be to locate these men and arrest them before the Texans also found them—and killed them. He thought that if Quayle's men did this, being strangers and already unpopular in the Ione country, Morton and Fisk wouldn't have any trouble at all fanning a range-war into existence.

Thinking like this as he rode along, Fulton came to the conclusion that now he understood why Big Jim and Buckley Fisk had acted so thoroughly out of character that morning. *They had known exactly what was going to happen today!* They had planned this stampede in advance! Their reasoning was elemental too; they'd deliberately schemed to get the cowmen involved with the Texans in a range-war which would not only discourage future trail-herds from crossing MF range, but also, since they'd both made a show before witnesses of being disinclined towards violence, they could not be shown up as the instigators.

What Fulton had to know now was who, exactly, had been in that band of riders which had hit the Texan camp. If he could locate just one of those men, and make him talk, he'd have his answers.

'Hey,' Ab said suddenly. 'Look yonder there; two riders closin' in on us with carbines.'

Fulton saw the horsemen and swerved to meet them. He was certain they were Quayle's men, and he was right. Both the cowboys, evidently put out as sentinels, halted when they saw Fulton and Ab heading their way. They sat with carbines balanced across their laps, waiting. As Fulton came up he called ahead identifying himself. The Texans sat like stone, their faces flushed and dusty from recent hard riding. As Fulton and Ab came down to a halt one of them squinted sardonically at the little silver circlet pinned to Fulton's shirt-front and said dryly, 'You're a mite late, Marshal, the damage's already been done.'

'Turn around and head for your camp,' ordered Fulton. The Texans obeyed in heavy silence, but when the four of them were passing around the sloping flank of a foothill one of them looked wryly around and said, 'Will got to town all right, I reckon, or you wouldn't be here. But where's Hud and Mister Quayle.'

'They're coming,' replied Fulton. 'And Will is dead.'

Both the cowboys looked swiftly at Fulton. 'Dead? How come he's dead?'

Fulton stared. 'Didn't you know he was shot?'

'Will—shot? Hell, Marshal, he was all right when he left here.'

Fulton considered those two dirty faces a moment then exchanged a look with Ab Slaughter who reached up, removed his cinnamon-coloured derby hat, scratched his head in perplexity and dropped the hat back

102

down again as he said to the Texans, 'Are you sure he wasn't wounded when he left you?'

'Plumb sure,' stated one of the cowboys. 'Hell; we stood around talkin' for a few minutes, then decided he should make the ride instead of one of us.'

Fulton, having assumed all along that Will had been shot during the attack upon the Texan camp, mulled over this fresh mystery. In order for Will to have been shot after leaving up here, at least one of those unknown raiders would have had to have remained behind to watch, and perhaps deliberately try to prevent word of the strike reaching Ione.

Ab was nodding. He said, 'Bob; that'd account for him bein' able to make it all the way to town with blood runnin' out of him like that. It sure amazed me when he walked into the saloon and fell down. I marvelled that any man could cover all that distance on a saddle horse leakin' blood like he was doing.'

Fulton heard a high cry on ahead and pulled straight up in this saddle, but one of the Texans, seeing this, said, 'One of our men, Marshal. They're out gatherin' up what of the critters they can find. Danged animals exploded in every lousy direction.' This man glumly shook his head. 'It'll take a week to find 'em all, and even them I'm bettin' we turn up at least a hundred head shy.'

'How many men were hurt?' Fulton asked.

'Three. Two by bullets and one with a

sprained leg when his horse went down under him. If Will's dead he'll be the only fatality.' This cowboy twisted to look far back. 'Sure wish Hud'd get here.'

CHAPTER ELEVEN

The Texas camp was a shambles. An indignant old man who was profanely and indignantly talking to himself at a little supper fire jumped up and stamped angrily around as Fulton, Ab, and the two rangeriders came up. He shook a big wooden spoon up at Fulton. This was the *cosinero*—the trail-drive cook—and like every one of his kind he was garrulous, testy, and out-of-sorts.

He said: 'So the law's finally come, has it? Well let me tell you something, bubba; ain't no livin' man goin' to get away with drivin' cattle through *my* camp! I want you to name me them fellers, Marshal! I want you to tell me where they went to, that's all. I'll tear off their cussed arms and beat in their skulls with the bloody end. I'll jump down their dad-blasted throats and kick their insides out. I'll—'

'Shut up, Cookie,' growled one of the cowboys as he swung down. 'Will's dead.'

The cook stood with that wooden spoon threateningly upraised, staring. 'Will—dead?' he croaked. 'Young Willie . . . ?'

104

'Yeah. The Marshal just told us. Someone shot him after he left here headin' for town.'

The old cook slowly lowered his upraised arm, turned and looked dazedly over where his pots were hanging from their pothook and aromatically simmering. As the others finished dismounting, led their animals over and tied them to wagon wheels, he said, 'You fellers want some coffee?' And stood there still looking dazed. 'Are you plumb certain it was Willie Short?'

Fulton, in the act of heading past to the fire, stopped in his tracks and stared at the old man. 'Short?' he hollowly asked. 'Willie *Short?*'

The cook looked up. 'Yeh. He was makin' his second drive this year. He lived near us down along the south Pecos. His sister an' young Tony—they're sort of bespoken.'

Fulton sagged. 'No,' he whispered. 'Not her *brother.*'

'You know Barbi?' asked the cook, looking puzzled about this. 'How would one of you Oklahoma boys know the Shorts from down along the Pecos?'

But Fulton didn't answer. He went on over where Ab was already filling several tin cups from the big old dented pot and dropped down cross-legged feeling drained dry. The others were also sitting like that. For a while none of them had anything to say. But when the cook ambled over one of the Texans squinted up at him. 'Any of the others been back?' he inquired.

The cook waggled his head. 'Not yet. But the boys in the other wagon are here. Lem's got a busted leg, it ain't sprained like we first figured.'

'You splint it, Cookie?'

'Yas. An' I made mutton-tallow poultices to draw the meanness out of the other two's bullet holes. Neither of 'em is hurt bad, just bled out a mite.' The old man looked at Ab's derby hat and town clothes. 'You a marshal too?' he asked.

Ab shook his head without answering, emptied his cup and stood up. He was the shortest man there. He walked away making a little circle and studying the ground. The Texans watched this for a while then one of them called over quietly, saying, 'We done already tracked 'em, mister, as best we could, but they weren't greenhorns. They let the cattle cover up for 'em.'

Fulton heard this and came out of his reverie to ask a question. 'Did any of you get a good look at just one of them?'

The cook and both cowboys shook their heads. 'They come out of the sun, Marshal, hit us hard and fast an' kept right on going. It was exactly like the Comanch' used to ride. One minute we were loafin' around camp here, the next minute all hell had busted loose, cattle were charging every which way, and those of us as could, got to our horses. The others run for

106

the wagons with critters bustin' through this camp like they'd gone wild. Everybody started shooting an' yelling.' The cowboy gave his head an exaggerated wag. 'Damndest thing I ever saw. Maybe some of the others fellers who're out trying to round up the cattle might've seen a face or two, but I sure doubt it. Them raiders knew exactly what they were doing, and believe me, pardner, they sure done it.'

The cook, returning to the tailgate of his chuckwagon, suddenly turned, cocked his head, and said, 'Riders coming.' As though this were a signal those two Texans whipped up off the ground and ran for their saddle-scabbards. Ab, returning from his little track-hunting foray, said, 'It's probably men from Ione.'

Fulton got up, flung away the gritty dregs of coffee from his tin cup, paced over and put the cup upon the chuckwagon tailgate. He knew who these oncoming riders would be and he was hoping with all his might that Barbara would not be among them.

But she was. He saw her the moment Travis Quayle, his beautiful daughter, his son and Hudson Marsh hove into sight being flanked by Joel Dunlap and Fred Whorton. She was riding beside Belle, her face as white as a sheet.

The day was nearly spent now. There were long shadows on the east side of things; the overhead heavens were changing colour and along the yonder slopes of Ambush Canyon was a sifting of evening's early haziness.

Fulton turned as Ab said, 'Look at his face,' and inclined his head towards Travis Quayle. 'He's cocked and primed an' I wouldn't want to be those idiots who did this to him.'

Ab drew forth two cigars, handed one to Fulton and bit down upon the other one himself. He afterwards held a light and remained there until Fulton, seeing the others all heading for the wagon where the wounded men lay, turned and said, 'Come on, Ab; let's use the last daylight scouting a little.'

They rode away without anyone paying them the least attention. They passed along northerly for a while, saw nothing but churned earth from the stampede in that direction, swung west and finally angled down southward, still without locating anything worthwhile. Ab clearly had not been hopeful right from the start. Fulton was hopeful but not expectant, which was just as well because, as that Texan had said, cattle tracks covered every other sign on the chewed-up plain.

'Might as well head back and listen to their talk,' said Fulton, and Ab began to frown. He had a saloon business in town to look after. Not that it hadn't gotten along without him before and couldn't get along without him now, but he was a businessman and remaining away too long made him impatient to get back. But he offered no immediate objection as

Fulton reversed his course and rode along heading back for the Texas camp, he just poked along with his eyes on the ground, which was fortunate, because before they'd gone a hundred yards on this new course he saw something in the fading light that caused him to say, 'Whoa,' to his horse. He swung down, stooped, picked up something that shone with a dull glow, bent over it, then grunted and passed this object along to Fulton.

As he re-mounted Ab said, 'I reckon we know now about where that ambusher was waitin' for the dead Texan to come along.'

The thing he'd handed Fulton was a fresh brass bullet casing. Fulton smelt it. 'Couple hours old,' he said, and twisted in the saddle to look around. There was a clump of spidery little bois d'arc trees close by. Aside from that this was open country for a mile in any direction. Fulton reined over to the little trees, got down and paced carefully ahead. Daylight was fast failing now. As Ab came up, halted and leaned from the saddle, Fulton dropped to one knee, minutely examined the dusty earth, and got up again.

'See anything?' Abner asked.

Fulton nodded. 'His bootprints. Here's where he waited. Stood here quite a while too, but he was nervous and kept fidgeting.'

'I'd have been nervous too,' opined little Ab dryly. 'If those Texans had stumbled on to him they'd have made mincemeat out of him.'

109

'He shot from here,' went on Fulton as he turned and ran a careful gaze on out to the place where Ab had found that casing. 'Then he walked out to see if he'd made a killing shot. While he was standing there looking after Will Short he automatically ejected that casing and levered up another bullet.'

'Why didn't he chase the Texan and make sure?'

Fulton shrugged, mounted and swung away. 'He could have been afraid to, or maybe he was sure Short would never make it on into town.'

'Never underestimate a Texan,' muttered Ab, and went back north with Fulton, neither of them speaking again until, in sight of the little cooking fire with its backgrounded wagons, moving men and tied horses, Fulton hailed the onward men to preclude someone with a nervous trigger-finger shooting first and looking afterwards.

When they got up there Travis Quayle and his son were standing clear of the others, waiting. Back yonder Hudson Marsh and the others, but not Barbara nor Belle, were at the fire soberly watching Fulton and Slaughter approach.

Travis Quayle waited until Fulton dismounted, then he said, 'It had to be those damned cattlemen of yours, Marshal.'

Fulton looked into that rugged, savage face and said, 'Any of your men see a face well

110

enough to make a positive identification?'

Tony spoke up, saying, 'No. We asked. They say it happened too fast. Marshal; Will wasn't shot out here. Someone drygulched him on his way to town with the news.'

Fulton nodded. 'I know, Tony.' He held out the brass casing. 'I know where he waited and where he fired from.'

Travis Quayle grabbed that casing and glared at it, then he handed it back. 'I'm ridin' over to have a talk with Morton and Fisk,' he said. 'I want to know the reason for that attack. I also want the name of the man who killed Willie Short.'

Fulton shook his head. 'You stay away from Morton and Fisk. I'll talk to them. I'll also talk to their riders and their neighbours.'

Quayle softly snorted. 'Talk,' he snarled. 'The time is past for talking, Marshal. No one hits a herd of mine, kills a rider of mine and shoots up three other men in my camp, and afterwards just *talks*.'

Fulton braced into the older man's icy glare and said once more, 'You stay away from Morton and Fisk, Mister Quayle. I'm not asking you, I'm *telling* you!'

Tony looked anxiously at his father. 'Hud said there were almost forty of 'em when he met 'em out here. Counting you'n me all we've got left is six men able to ride and shoot.'

Travis Quayle said savagely, 'Six to start with, Tony, but we can hire fifty more. I've got enough in my moneybelt for that with plenty left over.'

Ab Slaughter looked quickly up, his expression showing strong disapproval of this statement. But Ab said nothing; just stood there grimly chewing on his dead cigar.

Fulton's expression didn't change towards the elder Quayle, neither did his feelings when he said, 'You make a war out of this and I'll lock you up along with every man who rides with you.' Then he took a little of the sting out of that ultimatum by saying, 'I'll find out who did this. I'll also see that they pay in full for it, too. In the meantime you'd better concentrate on finding your cattle.' He turned and would have walked away but Travis Quayle stopped him.

'You're asking me to overlook the deliberate murder of one of my men, Marshal, not to mention everything those raiders have done. Well; I don't aim to do that, not by a damned sight, and no lawman, not even a Federal U.S. Marshal, will change that, law or no law. I'm going to see Morton and Fisk and every man who was in your office this morning. *I want the killer of my rider!*'

Fulton stood and exchanged a long, hard gaze with Travis Quayle, then, without another word he turned, stepped up over leather and hauled his animal around. Ab Slaughter did the same, but Ab looked back once before they were separated from the Texans by the settling gloom of night. Ab still had that fuzzy stub of a cold cigar clamped in his teeth.

Fulton went back to the spot where they'd found that Winchester casing, but he didn't halt, he simply slowed and studied as much of this spot as the gloom permitted before passing on towards Ione. When Ab asked what he had in mind Fulton said, 'Why did they station that man down here to shoot the messenger, Ab?' Then he answered this by saying, 'Because they had a long way to ride and needed as much of a head-start as they could get.'

Ab shook his head. 'All he had to do was knock down the horse, Marshal. He didn't have to shoot the rider.'

Fulton had no comment to make about this, and in fact Ab hadn't expected any because he knew the answer to that as well as Fulton did. Some men killed when it wasn't necessary to, the same as some men lied when they didn't have to.

It was full dark before they hove into sight of Ione's little orange lights. The night was balmy and pleasant with a pleasing fragrance. There was a high rash of pale stars and a crooked old moon floating along on its eternal orbit. Ione shown up as a random series of little bright squares cast loosely down upon the velvet horizon.

They were within hearing distance of the town when Ab said, 'You figure to ride out and talk to Morton?'

Fulton nodded. 'I figure to take a few cans of sardines too, Ab, and sit atop a hill out there. Travis Quayle seemed to me to be a man of his word. I know how he feels. At least I *think* I know, I know something else, he isn't going to catch Big Jim or Buckley Fisk off guard. They'll be waiting, watching—hoping he'll do something like that.'

Ab nodded and muttered, 'Yeah. Those two won't be caught napping. Not by Travis Quayle or anyone else. But if Quayle tries anything—I pity his heirs.'

CHAPTER TWELVE

Fulton left town ahead of the sun the following morning. He had his saddlebags aft of the cantle, his carbine slung under his right fender, and a night of solemn thinking behind him.

He was convinced that Big Jim was behind that strike at the Texas herd. Not simply because it would put MF's neighbours on the defensive and in trouble with the Texans, but also because that was the way MF had operated in former times when someone had crossed them. All those tales he'd heard of settlers disappearing coincided with this same kind of a slashing attack upon unsuspecting men. Even the way that attack was

114

engineered—with the sun in the eyes of the attacked men—belonged to an earlier time; an era when whiteskins and redskins used the same stratagems.

He rode along deploring the senselessness of it, but satisfied that sooner or later, with Quayle's herd or some other herd, it would have happened anyway.

He also probed for some shortcoming on his own part which might have helped this to happen, and decided that if there was one, then it had to be that he'd neglected to appreciate that Big Jim Morton and Buckley Fisk were, as he and Ab had discussed in the saloon two days before, the same fierce and cold-blooded men they had been a quarter century earlier.

He was within sight of MF's wagonroad by sunup, and later, he spotted the unpainted, weathered big old durable ranch buildings. Here, he also spotted something else; a lone horseman sitting perfectly motionless a mile off watching Fulton. He made a face about that; if Big Jim had ever given himself away this putting a guard out to watch for riders who might be hostile, was the best indication of it Fulton had yet encountered.

And yet, two hours later when he crossed MF's yard towards the main house, he saw Morton and Fisk sitting over there on the porch watching him, and looking as cool and unconcerned as any two innocent men could have looked. In fact, as he dismounted and tossed his reins over the hitchrack before the house, Big Jim got up out of his chair, lazily smiled, and lazily walked over to the porch edge to say, 'By golly, Marshal, you must've gotten up before breakfast this morning.'

Buckley still sat back there in porch shade looking as impassive and surly as ever. Even after Fulton stepped up on to the porch Buckley still showed nothing in his eyes or upon his face, although he gravely nodded.

'You had dinner yet?' asked Big Jim. 'Me'n the boys just finished before you rode in but I think the cook'd still have something left.'

Fulton said, 'No thanks,' eased down upon a porch stringer with one leg dangling, and considered those two. 'That trail-herd was raided yesterday, Jim. Some men busted out of Ambush Canyon, shot up three Texans and stampeded Quayle's cattle to hell and back.'

Morton's eyebrows crawled upwards, his mouth dropped open, he was the epitome of purest astonishment. Buckley Fisk sat there showing nothing, no surprise, no particular interest, but Fulton had never seen Buckley show any interest anyway.

Big Jim breathed a long, 'No . . . !'

Fulton waited for all this real or feigned shock to pass, then swung his dangling leg back and forth as he said, 'I forgot to mention that the raiders left a man south of the canyon a couple of miles, and when one of those Texans

116

went charging past towards town, that ambusher shot him.'

Now Buckley Fisk's eyes flickered a little. He said, 'Kill him, Marshal?'

'Not on the spot, no. But he died in Ab Slaughter's back room at the saloon right after he told us what happened. And that makes it murder, Buck.'

Fisk shrugged. 'You rode all this way just to tell us about that?' he said coldly.

'Not quite,' said Fulton, concentrating upon Fisk. 'I also wanted to know if all you fellers stayed together and came straight on back from town yesterday.'

'Sure did,' stated Fisk. 'The others came here an' Jim treated 'em all to a drink before they headed for their home places.' Fisk ironically smiled. 'Ride over and ask around, Marshal.'

'I figure to, Buck,' retorted Fulton quietly. 'That's why I got an early start this morning.'

Big Jim, watching Fulton and his pardner, broke in now to say, 'I was afraid something like this might happen. The boys been pretty fired up these past few days.'

Fulton looked sardonically around. 'Got any ideas, Jim? This isn't just a case of stampeding a trail-herd, this is a case of out-and-out murder.'

But Big Jim sat down and spread out his hands palms up. 'Lord no, Marshal. Like I said in your office yesterday; I'm a peaceable man.

117

I'd have been for lettin' that herd pass without payin' a thin dime to keep there from bein' any violence.'

'Yes, I heard that,' said Fulton dryly, and watched Big Jim's oily, coarse face. He had gotten all from these two he would get. He stood up, stepped over to the edge of the porch and said, 'Jim; you met Travis Quayle yesterday. He's not a man to fool with.'

Buckley Fisk made a little derisive sound in his throat but when Fulton looked around, Buckley was gazing straight ahead out over the yard looking uninterested again.

'He thinks you're involved, Jim,' said Fulton, stepping down, moving slowly over to stop beside his horse. 'He might come here to talk to you.'

'Let him come,' said Fisk meaningfully. 'Him and his lousy Texans. Let 'em come.'

Fulton ignored that and kept gazing at Big Jim. 'Don't let anything happen, Jim,' he warned. 'He's pretty upset about those wounded men and that dead one; you see, the dead one is the brother to the girl who married Travis Quayle's son in Ione yesterday.'

'Oh, hell,' snarled Buckley Fisk, standing up and looking tired of all this conversation. 'You know what I think, Fulton? I think instead of that badge they should've given you an apron and a little old grandmaw's rockin' chair!'

Buckley turned, stepped around Big Jim's chair and was five feet from the front door when Fulton moved. He never left the impression that he was a man capable of swiftness, yet he crossed over behind Buckley Fisk in two jumps and before Big Jim could even struggle up out of his chair Fulton said, 'Buck!' And when Fisk turned Fulton swung straight from the shoulder. The sound of that fist striking was the same sound a sledging maul made upon the head of a pole-axed steer. Buckley's feet left the ground by a clean three inches, he crashed backwards, struck the wall with a crash that made windows shake in their sockets, and he crumpled into an unconscious heap.

Fulton whirled and pressed his gun-muzzle into Big Jim Morton's gut. Jim had his own weapon half out. He froze like that, his eyes big, his face filling with dark colour.

'Take your hand off it,' said Fulton quietly. When Jim obeyed Fulton holstered his own weapon and he smiled straight into Big Jim's eyes. 'When he comes around tell him that's for yesterday. Tell him something else too; the next time I'll knock out half his teeth. And Jim—when I'm riding out of the yard, if you try a backshot, be sure the first one's plumb centre, because if it isn't you'll never fire the second one.'

Fulton stepped past, returned to his horse's side, caught up the reins, stepped up, settled across his saddle and exchanged a cold, black stare with Big Jim Morton, then turned and

119

rode leisurely across the yard. At the bunkhouse four men were standing there rooted; they had seen Fisk go down and they'd afterwards seen Fulton make that dazzling draw. They looked out at him as he rode past as though he were a total stranger.

At the barn doorway several other MF cowboys stood soberly watching, too. Not a one of those men nodded or spoke or even acted like they knew how to do either.

Fulton rode northwestward. When he was a long way out he swung to look back. MF's yard was empty; no one was coming after him. He settled forward again, raised his right fist and minutely examined it; the knuckles were sore, there was a small skinned place, but no swelling showed so he slouched along opening and closing the fingers to keep them limber, and later on he didn't keep on heading in the direction of Carleton Whitney's place at all, he instead swung eastward and made for a tree-topped knoll which would command an excellent view in the direction the Texans would come, if they *did* come.

He put his horse in among the trees atop that little hill, took some food from a saddlebag, sat down and slowly ate. He wasn't particularly hungry but eating helped kill time.

Once he saw three MF riders lope northward side by side. He watched those men as long as they were in sight and thought they were heading for Whitney's place. If that was so and they found that Fulton hadn't been there, there would be some head-scratching.

Later, Big Jim and two other MF riders rode westerly out over the range as though going out to look at cattle. Buckley Fisk evidently wasn't going to leave the ranch this morning, which made Fulton smile. He felt no great animosity towards Fisk, just the constant dislike he'd always felt. He had no regrets about what he'd done either; Fisk had been asking for that for a long time; he'd never been courteous to Fulton, had always acted as though he held Federal lawmen in particular contempt.

Fulton raised his right hand, worked the fingers and faintly smiled to himself. Perhaps now Buckley Fisk would still dislike lawmen, but Fulton was willing to bet he'd be a little more careful around them. Fulton lowered the hand; he'd also be a little more watchful around Fisk too; he wasn't the sort to forget that Fulton had knocked him senseless. Neither was Big Jim Morton.

The morning wore along. He saw a little bunch of cattle ambling along, mostly she-stock with young calves, and he saw a band of loose horses flash by with the bright sunlight striking hard against their shiny coats. He also saw a little faint sifting of dust far out northeastward, and he concentrated upon this until, some time later, he made out the riders, six of them, swinging along.

He sighed, feeling resigned to facing those oncoming men. There were all kinds of fools in this world, but the greatest fool was the man who, in a strange country with no more than a half dozen men, thought he could right a wrong with six guns in a place where the first killing would raise up at least six times that many other guns, in opposition.

One thing about anger, it blacked-out reason. Travis Quayle was a smart man and a successful one. In a business transaction he'd never think of bucking odds of six to one. Yet here he was now, riding towards MF doing exactly that and in a way that could wipe him out along with his son and all his remaining riders. Fulton got up, dusted off and stood a moment watching sunlight reflect bitterly off gunmetal. Odd thing about anger; even when it seemed justified, it still worked against the man who let it rule him.

He mounted up, turned and went anglingly down off his little hill, and although his shrewdness was paying off—the Texans were coming as he'd figured they might—he felt no elation at all. He liked these people, and yet he had to oppose them. In their eyes this would put him on Morton's and Fisk's side, and he liked that even less.

He struck the flat country below and set his course to intercept Quayle. A few minutes after he was out in the open they obviously saw him coming because they slowed to a walk and

122

began fanning out. In this way they would make a curving arc and have him under all their guns when they all met out there; it was an old manoeuvre but a tried and true one. He ignored it thinking it was only a precaution, thinking there would be no shooting anyway, and rode right up towards Travis Quayle who was in the centre of that slightly hooked line.

Travis halted, dropped his hands to the saddlehorn and looked steadily from beneath his flat hatbrim as Fulton also halted, with twenty feet between them. Tony was beside his father but with about eight feet between them. On Travis Quayle's left sat Hudson Marsh, about the same distance separating them. The others, true to common range tactics, were spread out the same way with the farthest men curving inward.

'I told you not to try it,' said Fulton evenly, giving the elder Quayle look for look. 'Now this is as far as you go. Say what you've got to say to me, then turn around and go back.'

Quayle shifted in his saddle. He looked beyond Fulton and he said coolly, 'This is a free country, Marshal. There's no law I ever heard of that says one man can't ride over and talk to another man.'

Fulton said right back, 'There's no law, Mister Quayle. Just leave these men here, shuck that gun you're wearing, and I'll go back to MF with you. Then you can talk, but you're not going to find Big Jim at home. I saw him ride out a half hour back. Fisk is at the ranch though, if you want to see him, but I'll tell you right now Buckley Fisk doesn't do the thinking for MF, Big Jim does. All Fisk can do is use a gun.'

Travis Quayle sat there gazing steadily at Fulton. The others were also silent and unmoving. Finally Quayle said, 'Why don't you just step aside, Marshal. Go for a little ride somewhere?'

Fulton shook his head at Quayle. 'You wouldn't stand a chance. MF has ten rough men plus Fisk and Morton and all their neighbours. You throw one bullet down in that yard and by tomorrow Miss Barbara would be burying her husband and Miss Belle would be burying her paw.'

'I think not,' said the big, craggy Texan. 'Or if it came to that, there'd be a lot of other graves alongside us, Marshal.'

'That's a foolish statement to make, Mister Quayle. What good would it do Barbara or Belle—or the kinsmen of these men with you—to know that some strangers had also died? None at all. Now turn around and head back.'

'I lost a man yesterday, Marshal. I've also got three hurt ones back at my camp.'

'I'm plumb aware of that, Mister Quayle,' said Fulton. 'Now let me tell you something. You try taking the law into your own hands, and I'll either bury or lock up every man

124

among your crew, including you and Tony.'

Quayle said: 'Alone, Marshal?'

And Fulton wagged his head at the big Texan. 'No sir, not alone. I'll deputise two hundred local men and come after you and keep after you until it ends just like I told you—dead or locked up.'

Tony Quayle spoke for the first time. He said, 'Marshal; will you put the same amount of work into findin' the men who hit our herd as you'd put into running us down?'

Fulton looked over at the younger Quayle. 'You've got my word for that,' he said. 'But every hour I have to waste keepin' an eye on you fellers, takes just that much time away from the other job.'

'Let's head back, paw,' said Tony to his father, and turned his horse.

Travis Quayle sat a moment longer regarding Fulton, then he too turned, all of them turned, and rode slowly back the way they'd come.

CHAPTER THIRTEEN

Every peace officer had his own method of working and perhaps Fulton's wasn't exactly orthodox but he adhered to it. He was cooling his heels at a table in Ab Slaughter's saloon nursing a nickel glass of beer when Carleton

125

Whitney came in the day after Fulton had turned back the Texans, beating dust off his pants. Whitney had three men with him, two of which were his own hired men, and the other was a neighbouring cattleman named Brody. Clarence Brody.

Fulton knew every one of those men. Whitney's riders were typical; they were resourceful men, tough as old leather, burnt berry-brown by the sun, and as loyal to the brand they worked for as rangeriders always were.

Clarence Brody was a dark-eyed, dark-haired, wiry man of medium height who was sociable and pleasant when sober, and slightly boisterous and troublesome when he'd been drinking. He owned the ranch adjoining Whitney's place, was married and had two children. He came to the Ione country the same year Fulton had also come there. No one knew anything about his life before coming to southwestern Oklahoma and no one particularly cared about it.

It was Brody who happened to look around and saw Fulton sitting over in a gloomy corner watching. Brody seemed startled. He threw Fulton a tiny nod and walked stiffly on up to the bar where he spoke from the side of his mouth to the others and Fulton, still watching, saw three heads lift and gaze ahead into the back-bar mirror where they could see backwards where he was sitting. Those looks

126

were revealing; something was troubling those four men. Brody then thumped the bar and called for drinks.

Fulton waited, sipped his beer and did nothing. Sooner or later one or two of those cattlemen would stroll over to his table. Other men drifted into the saloon, it was getting close to mid-day, rangeriders in for supplies as well as townsmen taking their mid-day break, came to Ab's place for a little refreshment. Two men from the liverybarn walked in talking carelessly and one said: 'That's why I quit workin' for the cow outfits. You get hurt an' you're so far from a town you could die before you ever got to a doctor. I've seen it happen. Besides, it's too lonely out at them places. Me, I like town life.'

The other man nodded, saying, 'Probably a horse fell on him.'

'Bullethole,' pronounced the first man. 'I seen 'em take him off the saddle and into Doc's place. He was bandaged like it was a bullethole.'

Those two passed on and Fulton, who had heard every word of their exchange, lifted his glass, emptied it, set it down and stared straight ahead where Whitney was leaning upon the bar. A strong notion was teasing him now. He wanted to talk to someone with a bullethole in him, and if what those two liverybarn hostlers had said was even slightly true, he was on the verge of a discovery. Still,

127

he sat there watching Whitney, Brody, and the brace of Whitney-riders, waiting, his thoughtful speculations running on.

There had been only one shooting affray that he knew of anywhere around—out at the trail-herd camp, and in that mess there had been a lot of gunfire tossed back and forth. Additionally, if someone among the westerly cattlemen had stopped a slug, unless it had been an accident at one of the ranches, there was an excellent chance that whoever was carting that lead around in him, had been in on the raid upon Quayle's camp.

Whitney stood over there with his head down toying idly with an empty glass. On either side of him stood his solemn companions just as quiet and pre-occupied. Elsewhere along the bar men were talking, laughing a little, and acting as men ordinarily acted in a saloon. Some were eating at Ab's free-lunch counter, but even these men were casually carefree. Just those four cattlemen over there were in different moods. Fulton sat on, never taking his eyes off those four and after a while Whitney straightened up, turned and started across towards Fulton's table. The others didn't turn to see where Whitney was going, but Clarence Brody struck the bar again and made a motion for three refills.

Whitney drew back a chair and straddled it. He nodded. 'Still no rain,' he said, and planted his elbows upon Fulton's table. 'Don't recollect it bein' this dry in springtime before.'

Fulton said nothing.

Two bearded freighters in heavy woollen shirts came lumbering through the saloon doors almost side by side. They were great, powerful men and looked enough alike to be brothers. They headed unerringly for the bar.

Ab Slaughter emerged from his office. Ab had on a fine pinstriped blue shirt with fancy sleeve-garters above the elbow. He looked out over the room, saw Fulton and Whitney, scowled irritably when one of those big freighters struck the bartop with an enormous fist, and turned to go wait on them.

'Anything new about that trouble at the Texas camp?' asked Whitney, leaning there steadily regarding the table-top.

'Not a whole lot,' replied Fulton. 'Yesterday I turned back the Texans on their way to MF.'

A little deep line appeared vertically between Whitney's brows. 'I heard tell that one that got killed was related to young Quayle's new wife, Marshal.'

'Her brother,' murmured Fulton. 'This was his second time up the trail.'

'They buried him yet?'

'Ab told me a couple of 'em came and took him out to their camp yesterday afternoon, late.'

'That was murder,' murmured Whitney.

'Sure was, Carl. A feller was waiting for him southward in a clump of trees. Shot him

129

without any warning.' Fulton fished in a pocket, brought forth that shiny Winchester casing and tossed it on the table.

Whitney stared at the thing with his jaw muscles moving. Finally he said, 'I need a drink. How about you—ready for a refill?'

Fulton nodded. Whitney twisted half around and called over to Ab, who nodded and started on around from behind the bar.

'Who'd you bring in to the doctor?' Fulton quietly asked.

Whitney didn't act surprised and he didn't reply until after Ab had given them their drinks and departed. Then he said, 'Ham Anderson. He had an accident.'

'Gunshot, Carl?'

Whitney threw back his head, tossed off his drink and made a face. 'Yeah; gunshot. Was cleaning his pistol an' it went off.'

Fulton left his drink untouched. He regarded Whitney steadily, his gaze sulphurous. 'You know,' he said mildly. 'If I've heard that story once I've heard it a hundred times, and I never could see just how it could happen. I've cleaned a lot of guns in my time, and they've always been unloaded first.'

Whitney belched, pushed the glass away from him and raised up off the table to lean back. 'I wasn't there,' he said, 'I don't know. But I reckon it could happen. Lord knows accidents with guns are common enough.'

'Ham Anderson works for MF. How come

you'n Brody to bring him in?'

'One of my boys come on to him north of the ranch. He was sittin' under a tree lookin' sick.'

Fulton dropped his eyes to his refilled beer glass as though he'd just seen it for the first time. As he lifted the glass he thought that Ambush Canyon and the Texas camp was almost in a straight line easterly from Whitney's place, and if Ham Anderson had been hurt in that fight, and had kept right on riding west, he'd have come out just about where he'd been found by Whitney's cowboy. Fulton drank deeply and set the glass back down.

'You ride down and tell Morton or Fisk you'd found Ham and were bringin' him to town?'

'Clarence was over separating cattle with me with one of his men. He sent a man to tell Big Jim and Buckley while the rest of us rode up there, bandaged Ham and started right for town with him. He didn't look too good, Marshal. The wound wasn't too serious but he'd bled out a lot. We figured if we wasted a lot of time takin' him down to MF first, then on into town, it might take too long an' he'd die.'

'And he told you he accidentally shot himself?'

'Yeah. Said he was riding along lookin' for MF critters up north and was wiping out his

131

gun as he rode, an' the damned thing went off.'

Fulton picked up his hat, dropped it on the back of his head and pushed back his chair as though to rise. But he didn't immediately get up, instead he gazed straight over at Whitney and said, 'Carl; you sure when you fellers left town day before yesterday after talking to Travis Quayle, that none of you split off and went north?'

The implication of this question was clear enough and ordinarily probably would have aroused resentment. But now nothing like that showed in Whitney's face as he nodded, not looking around. 'I'm sure,' he mumbled. 'We rode straight out to MF, had a drink at the house, talked a little, and broke up heading for our home places.' Whitney raised his troubled eyes. 'Marshal; we had nothing at all to do with that raid; I can swear to that on an open Bible.'

'I believe you,' replied Fulton. He got up, walked away without another word. There had been another question balanced upon the tip of his tongue but he'd deliberately neglected to ask it. Why didn't Whitney believe Ham Anderson's story about that accidental shooting? And Whitney didn't believe it; neither did those other men with Whitney who had brought Anderson in. It was glaringly apparent in their faces and actions that they didn't believe it.

Fulton walked out into roadway sunlight,

looked across at the liverybarn and the small, painted building one door southward which was the local medical man's combination office and residence, stepped down and crossed over.

It was said of frontier cow-towns that they'd reached maturity when they acquired a bank and a doctor. Well; Ione didn't have a bank yet and it had only had a medical practitioner one year, so, while it might be nearing maturity, it had only just begun to.

And the doctor was a young man fresh out of medical school. He wasn't a day older than young Tony Quayle, but he was very brisk and very efficient, so when he heard his roadside door open and close he came out to see who this visitor might be, and stopped in his tracks at sight of Marshal Fulton, wiped his hands upon a little towel he was carrying, and faintly, annoyedly bobbed his curly head up and down.

'I wondered if you wouldn't be along,' he said. 'One thing I've learned about Ione, Marshal. The best way to keep a secret here is to shout it from the rooftops.'

Fulton softly smiled. He'd run into this young man's sarcasm before. 'Is he still alive, Doctor, and what are his chances?'

'Mister Anderson? Yes, he's alive. But the answer to the other question is out of my hands. I've stopped the bleeding but he's unconscious. It's now up to his constitution. He's a healthy person though; I think he might

133

make it.'

Fulton strolled on over and looked past the doctor into his little clinic-room. He recognised the man lying there limply stripped to the waist, eyes closed, face grey-slack and whisker-stubbled.

He shouldered past the medical man, crossed to the table where Anderson lay and watched the wounded man's eyelids. There was no flutter at all; Anderson was unconscious all right. He turned, picked up the bloody shirt and held it out gazing at it sceptically.

The doctor watched all this from back by the door, finally finished wiping his hands and went over to stand with Fulton.

'This the shirt you took off him, Doctor?'

'Yes.'

'See any powder-stains on it, Doctor?'

The medical man looked and shook his head. 'No. Should there be?'

Fulton tossed the shirt aside and gazed over at the unconscious man. 'Yes,' he said. 'There should be. A man doesn't shoot himself accidentally with his sixgun at less than arm's length and not get powder burned.'

Fulton walked over, lifted Anderson's sixgun from its holster, opened the gate and spun the cylinder, watched the cartridges flick past, then closed the gate and pushed Anderson's pistol into his own waistband. He smiled flintily. 'Another thing you might be interested in knowing, Doc; if Anderson had shot himself with this gun he'd have to have drilled four holes in himself—This gun has been fired five times without being reloaded.'

The doctor stood there beginning to frown up at Fulton. After a moment of quiet thought he said, 'I see. The men who brought him in said it was an accident. You don't believe it was.'

'I *know* it wasn't, Doc. But when Anderson comes around don't tell him that. Don't tell him I was here.'

'All right. But what'll I do with him after he comes around?'

'He can't walk can he, or ride?'

'Certainly not. He'll be doing well if he holds up his head.'

'Then just make him comfortable an' I'll be back to see him sometime today.'

Fulton left the doctor's building, halted out upon the sidewalk and looked right and left. Ione was quiet and peaceful in the afternoon sunlight. Across the road stood four men in quiet conversation out front of Ab's saloon. They were Whitney, Brody, and Whitney's two cowboys. Fulton regarded them for a long moment then started on over. They stopped speaking and gravely watched him approach. He thought he knew how they felt and what they'd been discussing. Being implicated, even accidentally, in a murder, was no joking matter.

135

CHAPTER FOURTEEN

Fulton said to Whitney's two rangeriders, 'Go on back inside and buy yourselves another beer. I want to talk to your boss and Mister Brody.'

The cowboys hesitated, gazing at Whitney, when he nodded they did as Fulton had asked, turned abruptly and re-entered Ab's place.

Fulton gazed sardonically at the two cattlemen. Both had been at that meeting with Travis Quayle. Both had ridden out of town with Morton, Fisk, and the other westerly ranchers. He said, 'I'll put it straight up to you both: Ham Anderson didn't shoot himself and you know it.'

Brody's dark gaze turned uneasy, he gazed past Fulton towards that little painted building across the road but he said nothing. Whitney scuffed his feet and looked down. Standing like that he said softly, 'It didn't seem likely that he shot himself. Still, that's what he told us an' we let it go at that.'

'Carl,' said Fulton, 'where were your riders while you were in town at that meeting yesterday?'

'Workin' the range. That's what I told 'em to do before I rode to town with the others.'

'Do you know for a fact that's where they were?'

Whitney looked up, troubled. 'I wasn't with 'em, Marshal, so how could I swear to that?'

Fulton turned. 'How about you, Brody? You've got two riders. Where were they?'

Brody shrugged. This sharp questioning was obviously irritating him. 'Doin' the same as Carl's men, I reckon. I don't know. I wasn't there either, Marshal.'

'You know what I think?' said Fulton. 'I think you two have been used. I think most of the MF riders were among those raiders that hit the Texas camp, and I also think some of your men were with 'em.'

Whitney's troubled expression deepened. He and Brody traded a look but neither of them spoke. Out in the roadway several riders jogged past. One or two of them called a loose greeting to the cowmen with Fulton and waved. Brody waved back and Carleton Whitney acted as though he'd neither heard those men nor seen them wave. Finally he said, 'Listen, Marshal; I don't like this. I didn't like it from the start. It's one thing to turn back a herd, even shoot a few horses out from under the fellers who are forking them. But the rest of it—I don't like.'

'What *is* the rest of it, Carl?' Fulton asked.

'That murder for one thing. Stampeding that herd for another thing. And shooting up that camp hurtin' three men.'

'Who were they, Carl?'

But Whitney's dissatisfaction didn't go quite

this far. He scowled but he would not name any names. Neither would Clarence Brody. He alternately looked at Whitney and Fulton. He said, 'Listen Marshal; you got Ham Anderson. Let him tell you.'

'Does he know?'

'He knows,' growled Whitney. 'He talked a lot on the ride to Ione.'

Fulton considered those two. He could arrest them both for being implicated, for being accessories, but the idea didn't appeal to him for the elemental reason that if he locked them up, and afterwards showed up on the westerly range to arrest others, the raiders would think Brody and Whitney had talked, which would make more bad blood and perhaps instigate more murders. The best way to nip a feud in the bud was to keep quiet about one's sources.

He said, 'All right, Carl; whose idea was it to hit the herd?'

But Whitney only fidgeted where he stood wagging his head. 'Ask Ham,' he pleaded. 'Don't put Clarence or me on the spot, Marshal.'

'There's a good chance Anderson may die.'

Brody looked at Whitney saying, 'If that happens we could tell him, Carleton. If that happens someone's got to tell him; otherwise you know what's going to happen.'

Whitney slowly thought about this, and eventually he nodded. 'All right; we're goin' to

138

hang around town today anyway, Marshal, so if Ham dies without talkin' we'll tell you everything he said.'

Fulton accepted this but he kept thinking about what Brody had said: '. . . you know what's going to happen.' That sounded to Fulton as though there was more to come. 'Listen to me,' he said. 'I know Morton and Fisk are the ring-leaders and I know you two have figured out that you're being led right down the line by those two, and that you don't like it. But if anything else happens, boys, and you knew it without doing anything to stop it— then there won't be a damned thing I can do to help you because concealing illegal knowledge is as bad as condoning an illegal act. That's what the law says and it's also what I say.'

Whitney raised his head. He seemed on the verge of speaking when Brody raised an arm pointing on across the road. 'The Doc's beckoning to us, Marshal.'

Fulton turned. The doctor was over there in his doorway making brisk gestures. Fulton thought those gestures were for him alone so he said, 'You two wait here,' and stepped back down into the roadway on his way across. Behind him Whitney and Brody stood glumly watching, but the moment Fulton disappeared into the doctor's place, they turned and passed back into Ab Slaughter's bar.

It was getting close to noon now, there was a steadily increasing warmth building up in

139

town and a soft haziness building up over the far-away range. Ione was bustling about its routine existence, making its discordant little noises, and at the schoolhouse someone rang the lunch-time bell.

Fulton heard that bell mutedly from inside the doctor's clinic-room where Ham Anderson's grey lips made an odd contrast to his highly flushed cheeks and very bright eyes. The doctor bent slightly and straightened up again. He lifted his shoulders and dropped them. 'This is what disillusions physicians,' he said with what Fulton thought was pain and bitterness in this voice. 'I was being careful with you a little while aback, Marshal, but privately I thought he'd make it.'

'And now, Doc?'

The medical man gently shook his head. 'There's a furiously spreading infection, Marshal. He's going to die.'

'You called me over for that?'

'Partly. Partly because he's been talking. He's out of his head, mind you, but the things he's been saying are in context.'

'Whatever that means,' mumbled Fulton, and stepped still closer to the place where Ham Anderson lay with transparent perspiration upon his forehead and upper lip.

The doctor walked to a wash-basin saying over his shoulder, 'You'll see. He'll start talking again. Just stay there and listen.'

It was a long wait though, almost an entire

quarter hour passed before Fulton heard the feverish man say anything, then, when words finally came he had to bend close to catch them; they were slurred as though Anderson's tongue had thickened.

The doctor came over looking grave and also listened. Anderson was speaking to Big Jim Morton—or thought he was—and he was explaining how he'd been shot as he raced through the Texas camp by an old man with a flour-sack apron tied around his middle. He also told of shooting down one Texan after he himself had been shot. He mentioned the names of other men who'd also been in that raid with him. Four of them were not MF riders but all the others were. Then Anderson mumbled something which made Fulton stiffen. He said, 'They earned their money, boss. We all—earned it.'

After that Anderson begged for water and weakly twisted left and right repeating his request for a drink. The doctor went after some water and Marshal Fulton slowly stood up. He moved out of the way when the medical man came back, held up Anderson's head and got some water down him, then eased the dying man back down, turned and looked round-eyed at Fulton.

'I guess you were right, Marshal,' he murmured. 'I guess he didn't shoot himself.'

Fulton ignored that to say, 'Remember the names he spoke, Doc. You're my only witness.'

141

'But hell,' protested the doctor, 'you can't use an unconscious, delirious man's testimony in court, Marshal.'

'Not in court maybe,' replied Fulton, 'but Doctor, I've got a feeling this won't ever reach court. Remember everything he said just the same.'

The medical practitioner dumbly nodded and twisted to gaze downward. He looked troubled and also concerned.

Fulton went back out into the little waiting room, crossed to the door and passed on out into the bright sunlight again. Across the way neither Brody nor Whitney were in sight. He took one step down off the plankwalk then halted, hearing riders swinging in from the north. It was Travis Quayle and his six riders, all looking dusty and unkempt, sleepless and raw-edged. He suddenly remembered what Whitney had said about one of Brody's cowboys riding down to MF to alert Morton and Fisk about finding Anderson and bringing him on to town.

All he'd need would be for those two factions to encounter each other here in Ione. He had no doubt at all but that Morton, Fisk, and as many of their men and neighbours as they could round up, would also hit town shortly. Neither Big Jim nor Buckley Fisk would rest easy until they'd gotten Anderson away from where he might inadvertently, in his ill condition, say something.

The fact that Anderson had already said more than enough didn't mean too much right now, for as Fulton watched those oncoming Texans, he could almost taste the acridness of gunpowder here in his roadway.

Travis Quayle was in the lead. Behind him young Tony and Hudson Marsh rode together, and behind those two were Whorton, Dunlap, and the other Texans. Travis saw Marshal Fulton standing in the dust and reined towards him. As these two came face to face the rugged Texan halted his horse and said, 'Marshal, do you know who killed Will Short?'

Fulton didn't know so he shook his head.

'*I* know who did it,' said Quayle. 'That's why we're here, Marshal. To get you to ride with us and bring him into town an' lock him up.' Quayle sighed and gently shook his head. 'This wasn't my idea. I've known how to deal with *his* kind for more years than you are old. But Belle an' Tony an' even little Barbi—they say we've got to do this all legal-like.'

Fulton felt relieved. He said, 'That sort of restores some of my faith in folks, Mister Quayle. Who is he?'

'Buckley Fisk.'

Fulton ran this through his mind and began to perplexedly frown. 'I don't see how,' he said. 'Fisk left town with the others right after that meeting with you in my office yesterday. The others swear he rode back to MF with them. That's a long distance, Mister Quayle. No

143

horse living could have gone all that way to MF, then back to the place where Will Short was shot.'

'No *one* horse did, Marshal,' said Travis Quayle. 'You see, Hud's an old tracker; used to scout for the army. He back-tracked that ambusher straight to MF's barnyard. He also back-tracked those men who met with me yesterday. The same horse Fisk rode to MF wasn't the same animal he split the breeze with gettin' back up where he spotted Willie, and shot him.' Quayle fumbled around in one of his saddlebags,. drew something forth and tossed it down to Fulton. It was a horseshoe.

'Last night Hud pulled that shoe, Marshal, off the horse Fisk rode back to ambush young Will. Look at the markings good because on our way out to MF we're goin' to ride alongside those tracks Fisk made an' you can compare 'em.'

Fulton gazed past where Hudson Marsh was sitting, his cold, steely gaze steadily holding to Fulton. 'How'd you get this shoe?' Fulton asked.

Hud said: 'Got in there last night close to midnight with shoe-pullers, found the horse in the corral, and yanked that shoe.'

'And how do you know Buckley Fisk was riding that horse?'

Hud's square-jawed face showed the faintest of little cruel smiles. 'Real easy, Marshal; I waylaid the first man out of the bunkhouse at dawn, knocked him over the skull, took him out to our camp behind my saddle, and the six of us sort of prevailed upon him to tell us.'

'He knew Fisk rode the horse?'

'You'd be surprised how much he knew,' stated Travis Quayle. 'He even told us our cook got one of them; said he saw this friend of his named Anderson get it when Cookie was blasting away.' Quayle paused to draw his eyebrows inward and downward at Fulton. 'In Texas our lawmen'd have all this same information by now. In Texas they don't hang around the towns, Marshal.'

Fulton looked long at the shoe before he softly said, 'Put your horses in the liverybarn, Mister Quayle, then come back here.' He jerked his thumb over one shoulder towards the neat little painted building he'd just walked out of. 'I'll show you Ham Anderson, the man who got shot, and in case you're really interested, I already knew most of what happened at your camp and the names of nearly all the men who were involved.' He looked straight up at the elder Quayle. 'And I learnt it without leaving town—so maybe if your Texas lawmen have to do that same thing by beating their saddles, I'd say they're using the wrong end of their anatomies to think with.'

Fulton retraced his steps to the boardwalk, turned and found Quayle and his men

145

swinging down out in the roadway. 'I said take the horses into the liverybarn,' he called back.

Quayle scowlingly said, 'A hitchrack is good enough,' and started towards one.

'A hitchrack is *not* good enough,' contradicted Marshal Fulton. 'I'm expecting Morton, Fisk, and their riders in town any minute now and I don't want any Texas-branded horses out in plain sight for them to see. Now do like I said—take 'em to the liverybarn!'

CHAPTER FIFTEEN

Fulton waited until the six Texans came back from putting up their horses, then he took them all into the doctor's back room where Ham Anderson lay dying. The doctor was also there; he eyed these strangers with their hard eyes and lashed down guns, but he didn't say a word about their presence in his clinic.

Fulton asked the medical man if Anderson had spoken any more and was told that in fact Anderson had repeated most of what he'd said before. Fulton then told Travis Quayle to stay by the bed and listen; to remain there until Fulton returned. He then walked back outside again, crossed over to Ab's saloon and found both Brody and Whitney at the bar. One of Whitney's cowboys was with them, the other man was not, and Fulton swore about that. That other man had been one of those men named by Anderson as a participant in that raid on the Texas camp.

'Where did he go?' Fulton asked.

Whitney was puzzled. 'Just walked out back,' he said. 'Hell; if you knew he was one of them why didn't you arrest him before.'

'Because I didn't know it before. Now come on, the three of you. If he hasn't left town we've got to get him before he goes out to meet Big Jim and the others.'

They went out through Ab's rear rooms and into the back alley, but they didn't find Whitney's rider. They split up going north and south, and when Fulton and Brody, walking together, came down through a little pathway between two buildings back towards the main roadway in front of Slaughter's place, they came upon an unexpected scene. Ab was holding Whitney's missing cowboy at the hitchrack with his backbar shotgun. The rider was white-facedly staring at the cocked hammers of that murderous weapon in the saloonman's hands and he was talking a mile-a-minute in a frantic effort to convince Ab he hadn't been implicated in the raid. But Ab wasn't having any of it.

What perplexed Fulton was how Ab knew this man was implicated. He walked on up, pushed Ab's shotgun aside and motioned for Brody to disarm the cowboy. After this was done and some curious bystanders came up to halt and stare, Fulton said, 'Ab; how come you to be holding him?'

Slaughter grounded his scatter-gun, darkly scowled at Whitney's sweating rangerider and growled: 'He saw those Texans ride in and left a five dollar bill on the bar an' made a break for it out my back door. Bob; don't no man act that scairt unless he's got a real guilty conscience about something, and the only thing's that happened around here lately a man could get that upset about, just by seeing Texans ride into town, was that raid on the trail-herd. So, I snatched up my shotgun and loped after him. Caught him just as he came out between two buildings runnin' for his horse at the hitchrack—and held him.'

Fulton looked at the furiously perspiring cowboy, jerked his head and proceeded to march the man down to his jailhouse. He locked the man in a cell down there, pocketed his key and stood a moment gazing in.

'How much did Big Jim pay you?' he asked.

The dismayed rangerider looked out but didn't say anything right away. He licked his lips, rolled his eyes helplessly around, and shook his head.

Fulton said, 'Come on; I already know everyone who was with you anyway.'

At this point Whitney and the other rider who worked for him walked in, accompanied by Clarence Brody. The three of them paced down to stop nearby and peer in.

Whitney said, 'Why, Lewt? How did you ever let yourself get choused into doing something like that?'

Whitney's troubled tone brought out his cowboy's anguish in a swift rush where Fulton's impartial, cold question had accomplished nothing. 'For money,' said the rider. 'We each got forty dollars in advance, boss, an' that's more'n we otherwise make in a damned month punchin' cows.'

'But hell, Lewt; there was a murder committed,' said Whitney. 'Forty dollars isn't worth *that* kind of—'

'There wasn't supposed to be,' cried out the upset rangerider. 'Buckley Fisk said there'd be no one hurt; said we weren't to shoot high enough to hit anybody—only stampede those danged trespassin' cattle. That's all. And look—Ham Anderson got shot, and one of their fellers got shot too. Honest to gawd, boss, nothin' like that was supposed to happen.'

Fulton and Whitney exchanged a look and Fulton ushered the other three men back up into his office. As he closed and barred his cell-room door he said, 'Carl; it struck pretty close to home, didn't it?'

Whitney didn't reply. He went to a chair and listlessly sat down. Clarence Brody muttered, 'I need a drink.'

'No,' stated Fulton, turning. 'What you need is two new men, Clarence. Ham Anderson named both your riders as participants too.'

'*What!*' exploded Brody, whipping around to face Fulton. 'He didn't mention my men on the ride in, Marshal.'

Fulton shrugged. 'Maybe he got lucid enough to see and recognise you, Clarence, I don't know. Maybe he just didn't happen to mention those two names to you—but he spoke them to me, and the doctor was standin' there as a witness.'

'Lord,' whispered Brody, suddenly struck by something. 'One of my men went to MF to carry the message about us takin' Anderson to town.'

Fulton was unperturbed. 'I know; you already told me that. And I'll bet you a good horse MF and everyone they could round up is on their way to Ione right now to close Anderson's mouth.'

Whitney looked up. 'Marshal,' he said softly, 'they better not get here. Not with Quayle and his crew already in town. It could cause a massacre.'

'It could,' agreed Fulton. 'But I'm counting on you two, along with Ab Slaughter, to see that it doesn't come to that.'

'An' me,' spoke up Whitney's remaining cowboy. 'I wasn't on that raid, Marshal.'

Fulton looked steadily at this man. Anderson hadn't named him, but evidently Anderson hadn't mentioned any of his companions on the ride to town, and even afterwards when Fulton and the doctor had been listening, Anderson had neglected to name all ten or twelve men who'd been in on that attack. Fulton had caught only six names, but according to the Texans who'd survived the attack there had been about ten raiders.

Still, Fulton decided to allow this cowboy the opportunity to prove he wasn't implicated. 'All right,' he said. 'Come along, the three of you.'

Whitney stood up. 'Come where?' he asked.

'To meet the Texans. They're at Doc's place.' Whitney began to look distressed. Fulton, seeing this, said, 'Listen, Carl, and you other two men also. I don't know how many men MF is bringing here, but I *do* know it'll be at least ten, maybe eleven guns. There are only six of those Texans. The four of us will even that up a little—plus Ab and his scatter gun, and maybe the doctor too. It's going to take that many guns to hold MF from doing a lot of killing to get to Ham Anderson, and I think Buckley Fisk and Jim Morton would be willing to kill to shut Anderson up.'

'Too late for that, isn't it, Marshal?' asked Whitney's remaining cowboy.

'Yes. But Fisk and Morton won't know that. And besides, those Texans are fired up too. Now come on. And when we get in up there, don't say a thing, don't do a thing; just be quiet and watch me. If Quayle won't listen to reason, then we're going to be in a pretty bad spot

151

between his Texans and MF.'

As Fulton stepped along to the roadside door he looked at that cowboy, saying, 'Go up to the saloon and tell Ab I want him over at the doctor's place—with his shotgun. Make it fast.'

When the four of them hit the plankwalk Whitney's man cut away heading rapidly over across the roadway northward, towards Slaughter's place. The other three, Brody, Whitney, and Marshal Fulton, bore steadily along on their own side of the roadway towards the doctor's building.

Hudson Marsh was standing idly outside, his burly shoulders planted against the building front. He and Fulton exchanged a sardonic look. Marsh didn't just happen to be out here, he'd been put here to keep watch. Fulton walked on past with his pair of companions.

Inside, Travis Quayle and young Tony were in the other room softly speaking. They halted and stared hard at Whitney and Brody. The elder Quayle obviously recognised those two as some of the cattlemen with whom he'd met the day before down at Fulton's office. His stance as well as his look was hostile.

Fulton saw this and said, 'Mister Quayle; Whitney and Brody are going to help me keep the peace when MF rides into town.'

Travis Quayle's mouth drooped. 'A couple of sidewinders would help too,' he said, and Fulton turned cold towards the heavier, older

152

man.

'That'll be enough of that,' he said evenly. 'Neither of these men knew anything about the raid or the killing until this morning. They're the ones who helped me get what facts I've gotten so far. You'll owe them more than sarcastic remarks before this is over. Now let's all go on into Doc's clinic.'

'Why,' said young Tony, looking straight at Fulton from those slate-grey eyes of his which were so much like his father's eyes, and also Belle Quayle's eyes. 'It's no use, Marshal. Anderson is dead.'

Fulton took this without questioning it, but he stepped to the door and looked in where the doctor and four other men were gloomily standing above the sheet-covered body. He stepped back out again, sighed and nodded over into the mutely inquiring eyes of Whitney and Brody.

Travis Quayle was restless. He stepped around the others, opened the roadside door, looked out, growled something out to Hudson Marsh, got back a short answer, and closed the door again. He went to the other door and looked in where the dead man lay and where his other men were quietly talking to the doctor. He turned and found the men standing with him in the little ante-room soberly watching this restless activity.

'I don't like waiting,' he exclaimed, and frowned around. 'I want this Buckley Fisk an'

153

it keeps botherin' me that right this minute he might be riding in the opposite direction.'

Fulton shook his head at Quayle. 'You don't know Fisk. He won't run from you, Mister Quayle. Even if he knew he was suspected of murder, Fisk wouldn't run.'

'No?'

'No! Fisk and Morton are wealthy men. The fact that one scheme fell through isn't going to panic either of them. They didn't quite get their neighbours involved in a shoot-out with you Texans, which is what they wanted to accomplish, but that's not going to upset them too much, because they still might get that done. There are six of you and there will be at least—'

The door opening interrupted Fulton. Ab Slaughter came in with his riot-gun hooked in the crook of one arm. He had his cinnamon-coloured derby hat on and a half-gnawed cigar clamped in his teeth. He looked owlishly around, brusquely nodded and waited for Fulton to speak.

For a moment Fulton watched the door and didn't speak. He then went over, swung back that panel and peered out with a slow frown settling down across his features. As he eased that door closed and put his back to it he gazed straight over at Whitney.

'I guess we know who one of those un-named riders was now,' he murmured. Then he said, 'Ab; where's the cowboy who told you

154

I needed you over here with your shotgun?'

'Him? Oh; he said he had to ride out and fetch back some other fellers for the defence.'

Whitney looked astonished. So did Brody. Fulton didn't; he looked sardonic. 'Yeah; I wonder how fast and how far south he'll ride before he finds 'em?' Fulton said, then shrugged. 'He won't stop until he's down in Texas splashing across the Rio Grande down into Mexico.'

Ab removed his cigar, scowled and said, 'Him too, Bob?'

Fulton didn't answer that directly. He said only, 'We probably won't know all of 'em until MF gets here. Then we're going to need a lot of luck to survive long enough to write all those names down.'

CHAPTER SIXTEEN

Tony Quayle dropped a casual remark that caused Marshal Fulton's eyes to widen. Tony said, 'Belle and Barbi'll be waiting for us over at the diningroom,' to his father. The older man nodded to indicate that he'd heard, but he was obviously miles away in his thoughts and for that reason did not reply.

But Fulton did. He stepped up beside Tony and said, 'Why did you bring them to town, too?'

155

'We didn't,' said the youth, 'we sent them on ahead.'

The older Quayle scowled. 'Did you expect us to leave 'em at the camp when all of us were headin' for Ione, Marshal Fulton?' Then he turned to poke his head outside again for a look up and down the roadway.

Fulton had to concede that Travis Quayle was right; he couldn't have safely left the two girls at the deserted camp. But it also stuck in his craw that having them here wasn't likely to be very pleasant or safe for them either. He thought of detaching Ab Slaughter to go over and stand guard outside their hotel room, but he gave this up when he considered that Ab would spurn such duty.

Tony said: 'They're safe, Marshal. We got four upstairs rooms because we figured on stayin' in town tonight. They're in one of the rooms safe enough unless something happens in town and they look out a roadside window to see what's going on.'

'If,' said Fulton dourly. 'If.' He dropped his brows in thought. Something was going to happen in town all right, he was convinced of that, and he wasn't worrying so much about Belle or Barbi poking their heads out a window when lead was flying, as he was worrying about Fisk or Morton discovering who those two were, and that they were unguarded over there.

He went to the door, looked out,

shouldered past Travis Quayle to inquire of Hudson Marsh if he'd seen anything, got back a negative reply and shot a quick look at the overhead sun estimating the time. If the coming horsemen hadn't been too delayed by gathering their forces, then they should be arriving in town within the hour. The trouble with any kind of a close approximation was that no one knew how much they had been delayed.

Fulton decided to risk it. He turned, beckoned to Tony, and struck out for the hotel. He was starting on across the roadway with Tony Quayle a few feet behind when Marsh sang out.

'Hey Marshal; if you two get caught on that side of the road we won't be able to help you.'

Fulton's reply to that was brusque. 'That same holds true for Belle and Barbi. If you fellers had been thinkin' you wouldn't have left them over there.'

He and Tony hurried along, got into the lobby and found the place half full of anxious, curious people. The clerk ran up to Fulton wringing his hands. In a breathless way he said, 'What is it, Marshal Fulton; what's going to happen?'

'Maybe nothing,' replied Fulton, 'and maybe a gun battle.' He pushed on past and took the stairs two at a time with Tony behind him. They hit the landing and Tony headed unerringly for a particular door, struck it hard and when his sister opened it Tony jumped through.

Belle stood holding the door gazing up at Fulton, her heavy, arched eyebrows rising inquiringly. He stepped inside, shot a look over where Tony and Barbi were in each other's arms, and turned his back. He said, 'You girls'll have to come back across the road with us. It'll be safer over there.'

'I see,' murmured Belle, closely appraising Fulton's face. 'You're expecting the others aren't you?'

'They're coming, yes. I don't know when they'll get here, but they're coming.'

Belle looked past Fulton, her expression softening. She murmured so softly he had to strain to catch the words. 'Don't let anything happen to him, Marshal. Not now.' Then she took Fulton's arm and led him out into the gloomy, empty hallway, eased the door closed and put her shoulders against it. 'All right, we'll come with you,' she said. 'But let's give them a minute or two together.'

Fulton started to speak, checked himself, turned and strode down to the hallway's ending where a window gave an excellent view of the roadway below and the range beyond town. He stood there making his careful survey of everything in sight.

Belle came up beside him and also looked out and around. 'Nothing,' she said. 'It's as peaceful out there as it should be on a spring day.'

She was correct. There was no sign of riders, no dust, no moving specks far out; the land lay serenely undisturbed. He half turned towards her, saying, 'They told you who shot Barbara's brother.' She nodded, still looking out over the town.

'Why?' she breathed. 'Why did they have to kill, Marshal? We would have moved on.'

'MF wanted to stir up a fight between you Texans and the local cattlemen.'

'For what reason?' she asked, looking up at him.

'Several reasons. To make a fight out of this which would discourage other trail-herds from coming through the Ione plains, for one thing. To get the local ranchers involved in serious trouble, maybe even get some of them killed so that MF would have full control of all the range hereabouts.'

'Big stakes,' she said soberly. 'And now what, Marshal?'

He shrugged. 'Now it's not going to work out that way, Belle, but neither Fisk nor Morton will give up. They'll still make a fight out of it. They've always fought opposition the only way they know how to fight—with guns and men.'

'And if they lose?'

Fulton, looking into the calm depth of her eyes saw a deep streak of fatalism which matched his own feelings about things like this. 'A man knows what he's got to do and he does it, ma'm. He doesn't always think of the consequences, which is probably as it should be, because if he did, then maybe he'd run away, and that wouldn't solve anything.'

'Does perhaps getting killed solve anything?' she asked, watching the way sunlight turned his bronzed face a soft shade.

'Maybe not for the dead man, no. But he's not too important. It's what comes after him that's important, Belle. It's all the tomorrows that count. He couldn't be around to see many of them anyway.'

'Marshal; who would remember him—and his noble sacrifice?'

Fulton detected the irony but he had his beliefs and he said, 'No one would have to remember him, ma'm. That's not important. We don't always do things for a reward. We do them because we believe they must be done.' He looked out and looked back again. 'If every man thought only of himself I reckon we'd all of us still be livin' in caves.'

She smiled at him, a soft, tender smile. 'I know,' she softly said. 'I knew you'd feel like this too. But I wanted to hear you say it.' She turned to gaze on out over the town. He kept watching her profile, the lift of her chin, the roundness of her upper body, the way sunlight ran riot in her taffy hair. She pulled him, drew his thoughts away from everything else by her closeness bringing him to the verge of things

160

which were totally foreign to him. He reached out, dropped both hands to her waist and turned her back towards him. She offered no resistance and when they faced one another her gaze was steady and understanding.

'I never knew a woman like you before,' he said.

'But you've known women, Marshal. You're a handsome man. Women would *want* to know you.'

'Belle, you could stay here when the herd heads out for the Kansas plains.'

'Why? So I could bury you someday?' She gently shook her head at him. 'A woman can get over a little hurt, a sad little memory of what might have been, Marshal. She can never forget something wonderful that's been snatched away from her after she's had it. No; I'll go on with the herd.'

He swayed to her. 'You've already thought about this, haven't you?'

'Of course I have. It was like flint striking steel yesterday when I stepped into your office doorway and first saw you. Of all the men I've been around in my lifetime you were the first one who ever hit me like that, Marshal. Since then I've had lots of time to think.'

She lifted both arms, rested them lightly upon his shoulders, tipped his head downwards and stood up on her tiptoes to brush his lips with her mouth, but when he would have crushed her closer she dropped both palms to his chest and pushed. She dropped back down without lowering her smoky eyes, and made a soft little gentle sigh.

'That's what I meant, Marshal. That's how I knew it would be between us; rich and fulfilling and wonderful. I don't think I could stand losing it because of someone like Fisk or Morton with a gun in his hand.' She watched his face alter, become troubled and shadowed with his powerful, masculine hungers. She stepped clear, caught his hands, squeezed them both and let them drop. 'And this is your life, Marshal, which means no woman has the right to ask you to change it. If a woman *did* ask that of you, and if you did it, you'd never forget nor truly forgive.'

'Wouldn't I, Belle?'

She shook her head. 'No; because you're not the kind of a man who can compromise with yourself.'

The door opened where Tony and Barbara were. Those two came out into the hallway, looked right, looked left, saw Belle and Fulton up by the window, and started ahead to meet them.

Fulton was glad, as she turned, that the sunlight was upon his back and not upon his face. He and young Quayle exchanged a long look.

'You ready now?' Fulton asked.

Tony nodded, then he said an odd thing. 'Are you?'

162

Fulton's eyes drew out the slightest bit in a speculative way; why shouldn't he be ready? But he didn't say that, he simply nodded and stepped away bound for the stairway.

In the downstairs lobby that little band of murmuring townsmen had swelled to a considerable party of anxious folk, and as before the hotel-clerk came rushing forward to ask his questions, and also as before Marshal Fulton told him only that there might be trouble. But this time, seeing the number of people in the lobby, he raised his voice and urged them all to go home; to pass along word that trouble could come at any time and for everyone to stay indoors. Then, in the face of a cacophony of shouted questions he herded Tony with the two girls on out into the dazzling sunlight and on across to the doctor's building.

Here, he found the medical man in vehement argument with rugged Travis Quayle. The moment he entered the doctor turned on him saying fiercely, 'Marshal; I demand that you take these people out of here. My mission is to heal the injured, not support a quasi-revolution—or whatever's going on around here. I insist . . .' The doctor, seeing beautiful Belle Quayle and curvaceous little Barbi over at the door, let his wind run out slowly and let his angry words die away.

Fulton caught that look of dawning admiration and shrewdly exploited it. He said,

'Doc; I'll take 'em out. I'll take 'em all down to the jailhouse and we'll make our stand there. I only thought, having you among us, might save a few lives, is all. But I can understand you wouldn't want your place shot up by a bunch of—'

'No. No, Marshal. It's quite all right.' The doctor made a slight, graceful bow to the women. 'The jailhouse isn't quite the place, Marshal.' He beckoned to Belle and Barbara and turned towards the clinic door. 'Ladies,' he said, 'please come with me. My living quarters are back through here. You'll he perfectly safe there.'

As Belle moved out she looked inquiringly at Fulton. He nodded his head slightly, meaning that she should follow the doctor; there was a very faint twinkle in his gaze which she understandingly returned. Tony took his bride's hand and went along with her behind his sister.

Travis Quayle growled in his rumbling bull-bass voice as those four passed on into the clinic. 'I think you're wrong, Marshal. I think Fisk and Morton ducked out—left the country.'

Fulton shook his head at this statement. 'And leave a half a million dollar cattle spread behind? Not on your life, Mister Quayle. You don't know those two. They may suspect I'm after them, but they'll take a heap of convincing to be made to believe one man is any threat to them.' Fulton glanced around at the grim and dogged Texans filling that small room. 'Or that your remaining Texans are any threat either.'

Hudson Marsh poked his head through the doorway to frowningly look around until he located Travis Quayle. He said, 'Travis; it's past noon. How long we goin' to wait around here?'

Quayle looked at Fulton from beneath shaggy brows then said, 'Until they get here, Hud. Go on back and keep watch. They'll be along.'

Fulton waited until Hud had closed the door before saying, 'Thanks,' to Travis Quayle, then turned and went to one of the little roadside windows, of which there were two, one on each side of the door, where he stood with his back to the soft murmur of voices and gazed steadily out into the sunlighted, totally empty roadway for as long as it took to ascertain that Ione seemed entirely deserted. Except for a saddled horse here and there at the hitchracks, there was no sign of life at all; no pedestrians were abroad, some of the merchants had put up their shutters over glass windows, even the usual riders passing into and out of town were absent.

At Fulton's side the doctor had come up unobserved to also look out. He said, 'It's like a ghost town, Marshal.'

Fulton nodded without speaking. It was

165

indeed like a ghost town out there, but it wouldn't be that way much longer, he thought, for MF'd had enough time now to do everything which its owner'd had to do.

CHAPTER SEVENTEEN

But the trouble didn't come for another half hour. It was past one o'clock when it came, and even then it didn't occur at all as Fulton had expected. He and Ab Slaughter were softly discussing the long delay, both of them convinced that when Fisk and Big Jim Morton came, it would be with a hard, fierce rush down the roadway from the north, when they heard a solitary gunshot erupt from over across the roadway, and they, like every other man in that little room whipped upright turning towards the front wall. They heard something which was grisly portentous too, right after that gunshot; the sound of a man's body settling lower and lower down the outside front wall.

With a ripped-out curse Joel Dunlap sprang for the door, actually had a grip on the latch when Fulton's shoulder drove into him hard. Dunlap twisted half away and back again, his face made ugly by tension.

'They got Hud,' he husked. 'Fulton; get away!'

But Travis Quayle and young Tony stepped over to add their restraining efforts to Fulton's in wrenching Dunlap's fingers off the latch. The older man snarled at Dunlap. 'You fool; you couldn't get five feet before they'd have you too. Get away from this door!'

Dunlap was forcibly pushed aside. Fulton and Quayle sidled to the window and looked outward and downward. Marsh was lying out there slumped and lifeless, his hat beside him, his body strangely positioned into a sitting posture, his shoulders and head tilted back upon the wall as though he were accusingly looking on over where that unseen assassin had shot him. There was an almost insignificant little tear in his shirt-front squarely over the heart. Hudson Marsh was not only dead, he'd never seen it coming nor felt a thing. One second he was standing there bored with keeping the vigil, the next second he was dead.

Travis Quayle turned away as the doctor came across. He shook his head at the medical man, raised tortured eyes and made a similar negative head wag at the four Texans who were staring at him.

Fulton also stepped back, and just in time. A volley of gunfire exploded from over across the roadway smashing both windows and making the entire front wall quiver. The doctor involuntarily flinched and emitted a little gasp as he floundered backwards. The

167

Texans, unperturbed, turned to gaze as though they believed he'd been hit. The doctor's face burnt scarlet and he shook his head to indicate that he wasn't hurt.

Then silence settled, more hushed and strained than before, and to break it little Ab Slaughter, still with that frayed stogie clamped like iron between his teeth, still with his cinnamon-coloured derby canted rakishly atop his head, said reedily, 'They expected something, Bob. They figured you'd be waitin' for 'em. And they rode plumb out and around town from up north or down south, and come in from the one direction no one expected—from the east.' Ab bobbed his head up and down. 'That was good thinking on their part, you got to hand 'em that.'

Travis Quayle, standing slightly to one side of the northward window, looked venomously down where little Ab was hunkering with his shotgun. 'We'll see whether or not that was good thinking,' he rumbled at Ab. 'Wait until it's all over and count the bodies—then see who's a good thinker and who isn't.'

Ab looked up, round-eyed, at the big Texan. He hadn't meant anything by his comment. Then he dropped his eyes and strained to catch movement over across the deserted, bright-lighted roadway where his saloon stood, and as it occurred to Ab that MF was probably making his bar-room the headquarters for the attack, he began to swear with feeling. 'They'll drink my whiskey,' he muttered, 'and bust my backbar mirror sure as the devil.'

Whitney approached Fulton with Clarence Brody. Those two had been standing slightly apart from the Texans talking back and forth just before the first gunshot, and afterwards they became obviously distressed. Whitney said, 'Marshal; we don't believe Fisk and Morton could get all the other neighbours involved in anything as bad as an all-out attack on the town and the law. Call out over there, or let me do it; explain what we know, what Anderson said and what Mister Quayle found out; give them a chance to see what kind of a spot Big Jim and Fisk have gotten them into. Give them a chance to drop out before it's too late.'

Fulton turned as Whorton and Dunlap eased up to hear what Whitney had to say. The Texans were intently watching Whitney and Brody, their faces showing the slightest hint of dark suspicion. Travis Quayle also strode over.

'What's going on?' he bluntly demanded.

Fulton briefly explained and the big Texan nodded his head. 'All right,' he assented. 'Give them their chance, Marshal.' Then Travis coldly smiled at Whitney and Brody. 'I'd rather see 'em taken alive anyway; I want to see every man-jack who was involved even remotely in that strike against my camp—in prison or hangin' from a tree limb.' He nodded his leonine head up and down. 'Hail 'em, Marshal.

169

They'll maybe listen to you.'

Fulton looked around. Every man in the room was watching him, their expressions ranging from Ab Slaughter's look of hopefulness, to the murderous look in Joel Dunlap's eyes.

He didn't think it would work; didn't believe that those men would have gone along with the attack upon Ione in the first place unless they'd been convinced they had no other alternative. But what also occurred to him was that Travis Quayle's rough consent had nothing to do with the Texan's wish to avoid a fight; he thought he would have as much trouble preventing a mass-lynching from Quayle and his riders if he was successful, as he'd have trouble from the local cattlemen if he was not.

It was somewhat like being caught between the two granite surfaces of a pair of grinding wheels. He stood and looked into those uncompromising faces, then turned towards the window.

'Morton,' he called out. 'Jim Morton, this is Marshal Fulton. I want you to tell those men with you to put up their guns before there is any more killing.' He paused, heard his own echo, and called forth again. 'You men with Morton and Fisk—listen to me. Buckley Fisk is wanted for the ambushing of the Texan who was shot trying to reach town after the raid. Don't let Fisk or Morton talk you into doing

170

their fighting for them. Put up your guns and get out of town.'

Travis Quayle reached for Fulton's arm, half yanking the marshal back around. 'Don't tell them to leave town,' he hissed. 'Just tell them to—'

'Let go of my arm,' said Fulton coldly. 'I know what I'm doing, Quayle. Let go.'

The Texan let go, but he and Fulton exchanged a hard look. Quayle understood what Fulton had anticipated from the Texans. Understood perfectly why Fulton had told those cowmen out there to leave Ione. But he didn't say another word. As Fulton faced the shattered window again Travis Quayle stepped away.

Fulton tried again. 'You men over there—there have now been two murders. You've let Fisk and Morton drag you into something that could ruin you. Stop—before it's too late to stop. Clear out!'

Two nearly simultaneous gunshots exploded from over the louvred doors of Ab Slaughter's saloon. One of those slugs splintered the door near where Ab was crouching with his shotgun while the other bullet tore a long, dagger-sharp splinter of wood near Fulton.

Instantly, Ab cut loose with his riot-gun. Across the way his doors broke under the impact of those lead slugs and a man screamed. They saw this rangerider briefly when he staggered back drunkenly. Evidently he'd recklessly anticipated no return-fire because thus far the besieged men at the doctor's office had held their fire to a minimum. That was his biggest and his last error. He tumbled forward and fell half in, half out, the ruined doorway over there.

This man's death seemed to enrage the other men inside Ab's place. They opened up with sixguns and carbines driving Fulton's defenders to the floor to avoid being struck as bullets slashed through the walls, the door, the two shattered windows.

Fulton looked around. Tony Quayle was down on one knee returning that vicious gunfire in plain sight. Fulton yelled at him over the deafening gunthunder. Tony ignored this, shot his .45 empty, coolly stood up to walk away as he re-loaded, his place immediately taken by Joel Dunlap.

For nearly two full minutes this wild exchange continued before the necessity to re-load on both sides caused a diminution to set in. As the gunshots dwindled down to an occasional shot by both sides Ab Slaughter crawled away, put his back to a wall, removed his derby and poked a finger solemnly through a high-up hole from front to back. He then swore.

Fred Whorton crept up to Marshal Fulton. 'There's got to be more'n ten of them,' he said huskily. 'Got to be at least twice that many from all that gunfire.'

172

Fulton made no answer to this observation. He'd weathered gunfights before and thought that what had prompted young Whorton to believe there were so many gunmen over there was the noise of their steady firing, yet he knew too, that very often five men firing simultaneously could, and often did, incline people to grossly over-estimate their actual numbers.

Young Tony Quayle came up, got down and said, 'Marshal; maybe a couple of us could slip out of here the back way, get around town and come up behind 'em.'

'Sure,' said Fulton dourly. 'And that's where they'd cut you to pieces. No; we all stay in here. And Tony—remember you've got a wife now. Don't pull another dumb stunt like kneeling in plain sight of a window to fire.'

Fulton faced forward as Tony Quayle and Fred Whorton crawled away, back towards the others. By exposing only a fraction of his face Fulton could see out and across the roadway. But except for little lingering puffs of dirty grey smoke, there was very little to see. Ab Slaughter's louvred doors were lying shattered and the window of his bar-room had also been shot out. That dead cowboy was still lying over there where he'd fallen face-down, nearly cut in two by Ab's shotgun.

Down by the hotel doorway, which was recessed, two foolish townsmen were crouching, partially exposed, avidly watching the fight.

'Hey Marshal,' the unmistakable roaring voice of Big Jim Morton sang out. 'Send those Texans out and we'll let you go. Send 'em out, Fulton, or you'll go down with 'em.'

'You fool, Morton,' yelled back Fulton. 'You've just sacrificed everything you've worked twenty-five years to build up. These aren't the same days they were a quarter century ago. You can't settle things with a lot of guns any more.'

Big Jim's booming, harsh laugh sounded. 'We're doin' a pretty good job of it so far, Marshal. We'll riddle the lot of you—then what'll you say?'

'I'll say you're an even bigger fool than I thought you were, Jim, because the army'll come and a dozen more U.S. Marshals, and when they finished with you there won't be enough left to—'

Morton fired off three fast rounds driving Fulton to the floor where he rolled over, sprang back up and recklessly, wrathfully, exposed himself long enough to catch the winking scarlet muzzleblasts between Ab's place and the adjoining building, and empty his .45 at those flashes.

Someone over there cried out sounding dismayed and bewildered. Behind Fulton, Ab Slaughter gasped, 'By gawd I think you got him!' Ab wiggled up closer and out of nowhere came a bullet to take the entire top out of Ab's battered derby hat. Ab dropped down like a stone, rolled and stopped rolling less than a foot from his ruined hat. 'Lousy damned highbinders,' he swore. 'That hat cost me seven dollars imported from St Louis!'

The cattlemen across the road stepped up their gunfire again. They were systematically firing through the windows and through the badly splintered door. But Fulton, Ab, and Travis Quayle's Texans stayed well clear of those places allowing most of that lead to spend its slashing momentum against the farther-back walls. For as long as the initial volley-firing continued they did not fire back, but as soon as it began to dwindle again, as it always did, they took up the renewed battle with a vengeance, and now, after having survived the first exciting shock of battle, they were cool with their aiming and deadly with their firing. One of them caught a cowboy atop the hotel roof and dumped him forty feet downward head over heels into the dusty roadway with a slug through the skull. Another Texan, either Whorton or Dunlap, who were firing side by side and simultaneously, caught a shadowy shape whipping between two buildings outback behind Ab's place, and cut him down in mid-stride.

Fulton re-loaded and waited. He could see that the deadly return fire of Quayle's men was striking dread into the heart of those local cowmen over there. They were moving now, and there seemed to be less of them firing. It occurred to him that they might try getting around behind the doctor's building to attack from that quarter, or even to try and burn them out. But if they tried that, Fulton knew, the whole town would go up. The doctor's office was less than ten feet from the liverybarn on the north, and the general store on its left. All these structures were of wood; this time of year they would go up in flames with a wildness no bucket-brigade could ever hope to control.

He got up, stepped past the others and went on through into the little asceptic clinic-room. There was a door directly ahead. He made for it gun in hand, passed on through and found both Barbara and Belle standing there white to the eyes, looking at him.

'He's gone,' little Barbara said. Fulton stopped and looked at the girl, wondering. Belle came forward.

'Tony just left through the rear alleyway door,' she said. 'We tried to stop him but he said someone had to do it or we'd all die in here.'

Fulton lowered his sixgun staring past where another doorway was, its panel still slightly ajar.

CHAPTER EIGHTEEN

It took a moment for Fulton to gather his thoughts. He remembered young Tony coming to him with the suggestion that someone try flanking their attackers. He also recalled his short answer to that suggestion. Now, as he considered that ajar door and the faces of those two girls, white and stricken and mortally fearful, he knew what he had to do.

He gazed a moment into Belle's face, then brushed her arms with his hand and strode past. At the door he took a long breath, looked out, saw no one, twisted to motion the girls up, and said to them, 'Lock this door the second I step outside and don't open it for anyone. *Anyone!* You understand?' They nodded up at him. 'One more thing; if you hear anyone out here, call one of the others. Someone may try getting in from back here. Or they may try firing the building.'

He smiled gently at little Barbara. 'I'll find him, don't worry,' he said. Then he turned, put a cupped hand under Belle's rounded chin, swooped down and kissed her squarely on the mouth, hard, stepped out through the door and said: 'Lock it!' And he ducked swiftly southward towards the little dog-trot between that building and the one next to it, which was Ione's large and barn-like old general store.

Out here the sounds of gunfire sounded even louder, more pronounced and furious. He listened, tried to estimate where most of the enemy fire was coming from, decided in favour of Ab's saloon, then ducked out and ran crookedly southward as hard as he could leg it until he came nearly to the exposed byway of the first intersecting roadway.

Not a single gunshot had sounded around here, making Fulton think his other fears had been groundless. If it had occurred to the attackers to try flanking the doctor's place, no one had started out to do it yet, because if they had they could hardly have avoided seeing Fulton running; since no one had fired at him, no one had seen him.

He flattened along a wall, risked a quick peek around—and saw Tony Quayle flattened up along the main roadway sidewall of another building. He jumped on around and started to cry out. But at the same moment Tony broke away making a wild zig-zag charge across the empty roadway. At that exact moment the attackers opened up with another of their volleys. Fulton, straining for the running youth, was very grateful for that sudden intercession, for otherwise he was certain Tony would have been spotted—and shot down before he reached safety on across the road.

It didn't happen though. Tony got to safety over there, threw himself into the protective shelter of a recessed doorway and flattened over there.

Fulton breathed deeply in and out, gauged the fury of that raging battle northward, stepped out, shot a look off to his left and broke for the yonder side of the roadway. He was two-thirds of the way across when Tony saw him, recognised him, and, evidently surmising Fulton's purpose, sprang clear of his doorway and dashed between two buildings. Fulton cried out to him but young Quayle didn't even pause or look back. However, Fulton's yell was heard elsewhere, and as he landed down upon the opposite plankwalk a lead slug splintered the two inch rough planking under him, driving Fulton in a headlong lunge into that same protective doorway where Tony had been moments before. And that unseen gunman pinned him down over there by systematically slamming slugs into the outer woodwork.

Fulton fumed, waited until he thought it might be safe to do so, swung around and struck the door at his back. It flew open. Fulton had a glimpse of a white face, two bulging eyes, then he was past in a dash for the store's rear-alley exit. He got back there, lifted the bar, eased that door open and looked out. Tony was nowhere in sight, but neither was anyone else, so Fulton jumped out, darted northward to a horse-shied, glided inside this rickety building and tasted the sweat which ran from under his hat. Here, he took a breather, examined his gun, examined his clothing to see if he'd survived any near-hits, stepped ahead and looked up the alleyway.

Then he saw Tony.

Young Quayle was boldly trotting towards a band of horses being guarded by two cowboys. From a narrow slot between two buildings a cowboy stepped out as he re-loaded, called something to Tony, and young Quayle called back, made a careless gesture to this man and kept right on trotting.

Fulton's heart was in his mouth, but that cowboy stepped over, put his back to a protective building and dropped his head, concentrating upon re-loading. He'd obviously believed Tony Quayle was one of his companions in the attack.

Fulton left his horse-shed, passed over where afternoon shadows were thickening along some rear walls, got almost up to that re-loading man, and levelled his .45 as the cowboy casually turned and casually looked up.

The man's eyes flew wide open; his jaw dropped down. Fulton was less than twenty feet away. He said, 'Shuck the gun!' The cowboy didn't hesitate for even a second, he dropped his weapon and stood there dumbfounded. Then, as though struck by a frightening thought, he swung a frantic glance past Fulton as though expecting to see others back there also with their guns aimed at him.

Fulton moved up a little. He said, 'Where's Big Jim?'

The cowboy jerked his head backwards. 'Between them two buildings back there, dead.'

'Dead?'

'Dead as a mackerel, Marshal. Took one in the head and one through the brisket.'

'Where's Buckley Fisk?'

'In the saloon, Marshal, with them other fellers—the ones that didn't leave.'

'Who left?'

The cowboy lifted his shoulders and dropped them. 'When you yelled out a while back four of the ranchers pulled out.'

'Why didn't you?'

The cowboy shrugged again. 'Fisk said every man as stayed to finish the fight gets fifty dollars cash.'

Fulton moved right up. 'Turn around,' he said, and when the cowboy obeyed Fulton swung his handgun in a vicious short arc. The solid strike when that barrel smashed down across bone travelled like an electric shock all the way up to Fulton's shoulder. He stepped over the downed man, saw Tony Quayle disarming those horse-guards, and started ahead. He hadn't progressed a hundred feet when a man Fulton recognised as that cowboy Tony had beaten in Ab Slaughter's saloon for making remarks about Barbara, stepped out the bar-room's back door, looked over, saw

Tony, recognised him, and bawled out a rousing cry of alarm back into the saloon. As that man grabbed for his gun, Fulton fired from the hip. The cowboy turned, stared down at Fulton in purest astonishment, then pitched down off the little backporch into the alleyway dust, dead before he struck the ground.

Tony had turned at that outcry. He'd seen Fulton's shot one second after he'd seen his own peril. He made a little curt nod of acknowledgment over to Fulton, then grabbed his disarmed horse-guards, placed them both in front of him and started driving them over.

Three men appeared in the doorway above that dead rangerider. They didn't recognise Tony but they didn't have to; they saw the disarmed condition of their friends and swung to fire. Fulton blasted off twice, fast, driving lead into the doorjamb in front of those men. They hadn't had time to look along the backwall of Slaughter's building so hadn't seen the marshal. But when his bullets drove in beside them tearing apart the wood, only one of them got off a shot, and that slug sang high over Tony Quayle's head. Then those three men howled and fled back into the saloon.

Now there was no longer any chance of getting out of this alleyway without being fired on, so Fulton called over for Tony to forget his captives and run for it. But young Quayle was calm and steady; he shook his head and kept right on herding his prisoners along.

A bullet sang out from an overhead window. Fulton saw Tony flinch from a near-miss. For a second he thought Tony had been hit. When another slug came from that same place Fulton jumped clear of his protective backwall, raised his gun and broke someone's arm up there when the gunman pushed his hand out for a third shot. There was a great howl from up there, a sixgun fell, struck the porch, skittered over and tumbled down into the dirt.

Fulton was still gazing upwards when from dead ahead and on his left a man's rasping voice struck hard over toward Tony Quayle. Fulton recognised that voice at once. It belonged to Buckley Fisk. Evidently all the alarm out back had diverted Fisk from his forward direction of the attack across the road, and yet the gunman-pardner of dead Big Jim Morton did not step out where Fulton could see him. He remained back just inside the doorway.

He said, 'Step away from those two men, Texan, and meet me like a man.'

Fulton saw Quayle's head whip up, saw him stop at the cold menace in Fisk's voice. Fulton was about to cry over a warning when Tony said, 'Show yourself, mister, if you want it that way,' and Tony moved clear.

Fulton was afraid to breathe. Tony was fully exposed; worse than that, he had his sixgun back in that fancy cut-away holster as though to give Buckley Fisk an even chance at him.

Fulton's palm turned oily where he gripped his own weapon. Buckley Fisk, for more than twenty-five years, had survived half that many gunfights. His speed and accuracy were a legend in the Ione country.

He stepped right up to the doorway where Fulton could see him. Fisk also had holstered his .45. He stood there sardonically gazing down at young Quayle. Elsewhere, the gunfire was diminishing again. Out back there was an almost choking hush. Those two captured, disarmed horse-guards were like stone, craning around to watch. Neither of them had spotted Fulton yet, and now neither of them could have cared less that the U.S. Marshal was standing there.

'Any time, deaths-head,' said young Tony in his Texas drawl.

'You got more guts than brains,' rapped out Buckley Fisk, and moved with blurred speed. Fulton, who was trying to watch them both, didn't see Tony's gun clear leather and tilt upwards while still beside the youth's thigh, but he distinctly saw the red flash and heard the deafening roar as Tony fired. Buckley Fisk's gun was out and swinging. The older man's thumb was straining back on the hammer when Tony's slug hit him. It was a clear case of Fisk being out-drawn and out-gunned, and his face showed the complete amazement, the unbelieving astonishment, just before he went down, rolled across the porch steps and tumbled all in a heap at young Quayle's feet.

Now Fulton moved. He saw movement in the room behind, where Fisk had been and levelled his weapon to fire. But there was no need. The men inside there were staring down where Fisk lay as though not able to believe their own eyes.

Tony flagged at his captives. 'Go on inside ahead of me,' he ordered, stepping past dead Buckley Fisk. 'Don't try jumping clear either.'

The captives dutifully hiked on up into the saloon, and until Fulton distinctly heard the jangle of their spurs he wasn't aware that all the gunfire out front had stopped.

Without a word he joined Tony in entering Ab's back room. Side by side they pushed the dumbfounded cattlemen on ahead of them into the ruined bar-room where broken glass lay everywhere and the stench of spilled whiskey was almost overpowering.

The scene in there was astonishing. There were a number of dead men sprawled upon the floor and at least three wounded men were propped up along the far wall. There were three attackers left unscathed but at sight of Tony Quayle and Marshal Fulton what little remaining will they had to fight, leaked out. One of them tossed down his gun. The other two immediately followed this man's example. From over among the injured men a cowboy called over, 'Marshal; for gawd's sake get the doctor. I'm runnin' out of blood!'

Fulton looked around at the shambles. He gave each of the captured horse-guards a rough push over where the other three uninjured men were dumbly standing, and he said from the edge of his mouth: 'Go over and tell 'em it's all over, Tony. Send back the doctor and Ab Slaughter to keep an eye on these. And Tony—let Barbara and Belle know we made it. They'll want to know.'

Tony passed around the room, out the front door, and disappeared from Fulton's sight. As soon as he was gone Fulton put his sulphurous gaze at the surviving cowmen. He thought of a half dozen things to say to them but he didn't open his mouth until the battered Texans, with Ab, came walking in, halted, and looked at the wreckage. Ab let off a great wail as he surveyed his bar-room, his emptied backbar shelves, his ruined tables, chairs, and splintered bar.

'They'll pay for it,' said Fulton. 'We'll hold a public auction of their herds, Ab, don't worry.'

Travis Quayle walked over, put a wintry stare upon the survivors and said to Fulton, 'You can have 'em, Marshal. I wouldn't soil my lariat stretching their lousy necks.'

To his companions Fulton said, 'Give me a hand herding them down to the jailhouse. And Doc; see what you can do for the wounded.' He gestured for the defeated cattlemen to hike on out. With Whorton, Dunlap, both the

Quayles and one other Texan, he drove his prisoners down to the jailhouse. There, without a word being said, he locked them up, and there too, Travis Quayle, as he was herding his men back out of the office, turned and pushed out his right hand.

'You should've been a Texan,' he said. 'Marshal; I want you to promise me something—come over an' see me at the hotel tonight. I want to have a serious talk with you.'

Fulton shook and nodded and stepped away as the Texans departed. He removed his hat, flung it upon his desk, considered his little badge, then also took that off and threw it upon the desk, then he walked to the water bucket, dipped up a big drink of water and slowly drank it all down. As he was hanging the dipper back upon its nail someone said softly from over at the opened doorway: 'Marshal . . . ?'

He turned. Belle was standing there looking gravely over at him, her slate-grey eyes darker than usual, her long, heavy mouth lying closed with soft pressure, her expression quiet and gentle towards him.

'Come in,' he said, moving over to the desk where his hat and badge lay. 'I haven't had time to bawl your brother out yet, but I'll get to it.'

She came over close and reached up, bringing his head around to her. 'You're a big enough man to fill Hud Marsh's boots, Bob. If

187

you wanted to, you could do it. My father's going to ask you to take the job as soon as some of the smoke has settled.'

He faintly frowned down at her. 'You saw me take that badge off, didn't you, Belle?'

She nodded. 'I understand why you took it off too. Killing is bad for a man, even justified killing. That's what you were thinking, isn't it?'

He nodded. 'That's exactly what I was thinking. I'd better quit before it becomes easy and routine to me.'

'Will you talk to my father tonight, Bob?'

'If you want me to, Belle.'

'That's the *second* most important thing I want.'

'What's the first?'

She raised up, brushed her lips across his mouth, dropped back down and said, 'Any more questions?'

He solemnly shook his head down at her.